Praise for *Daughter of the Father*:

Peppered with vivid imagery, these stories bring to life Bible characters and situations. They speak lessons of hope, faith and peace to today's world.

Joyce Brinkerhoff
Board member, Society of Hope
Past President, Intercultural Society of Central Okanagan
Trustee #SD23, Board of Education, Central Okanagan
Director, Hope For The Nations, Mexico

Beverley Jane Whiting

Daughter
OF THE FATHER
AND OTHER STORIES

DAUGHTER OF THE FATHER
Copyright © 2015 by Beverley Jane Whiting

Printed in Canada

ISBN: 978-1-4866-0787-7

Word Alive Press
131 Cordite Road, Winnipeg, MB R3W 1S1
www.wordalivepress.ca

Cataloguing in Publication may be obtained through Library and Archives Canada

*This book is dedicated to nine wonderful women who
have encouraged and challenged me in my own faith walk,
and who I look forward to meeting one day.*

Contents

	Acknowledgements	ix
	Introduction	xi
1.	The Mission	1
2.	Destitute	9
3.	Desperate Measures	17
4.	Liquid Gold	27
5.	Daughter of the Father	45
6.	Food for Thought	79
7.	The Garment	91
8.	The Gift	105
9.	Wells of Water	113
	Afterword	127

Acknowledgements

In the preparation of this little book of short stories, I have received invaluable help from my son, Craig Whiting. Without his insightful comments, appropriate suggestions, and helpful corrections, I do not believe I would have had the courage to complete this work. I also want to say thanks to Annie, Ruth and my book club friends who gave me valid criticism and encouragement, as well as a special thanks to my editor, Kerry Wilson, for her helpful suggestions and patience in proofreading this manuscript. Most of all, I want to thank you, Lord, for giving me the material and the inspiration to write these stories.

Introduction

*"For everything that was written in the past was written to teach
us, so that through the endurance taught in the Scriptures
and the encouragement they provide we might have hope."*
—Romans 15:4

I have based the stories in this book on the true accounts of nine ordinary woman who lived thousands of years before our time, in the days of the Old and New Testaments. Their brief histories as portrayed in the Bible, hint at, rather than explicitly express, their inner turmoil and anguish while struggling alone to stay afloat and survive life's pummeling current. Hours of reflection on what it must have felt like for each of these women to hold desperately onto hope, while dealing with the raw pain of their imperfect lives, inspired me to write these fictional biographies. I hope I have done justice to their personal struggle, for the power of each of these woman's testimony is found in this courage to endure, despite bitter reality.

For the most part, I have remained true to the historic sequence of events as found in the Bible, often combining similar accounts from all the gospels where applicable, or choosing one above another. The one exception to this rule is found in the story of the widow in The Mission. Here I have not kept strictly to the geographic placement of Jesus' Sermon on the Mount, or the encounter Jesus had with the rich young man, but have merged these into the story of the widow, which takes place in and around Jerusalem in order to strengthen the effect.

And lastly, although these women lived long ago, I have not stuck exclusively to the language and imagery of their day, in order to help diminish the very real sense of separation that history and time can create from us today. This slight shift will, hopefully, leave an impression that any of these women could be the neighbor who lives next door.

The Mission

Silver-gold rays, those shimmering forerunners of dawn, filtered through the small slit in the wall as the deep darkness slowly lightened to paler shades of grey. I snuggled deeper under the goat hair blanket, wanting to linger in dreamland for a few more moments to relive pleasant times with Benjamin. Somewhere in the distance a rooster crowed loud and long in a resolute effort to display his manhood to his many chicks. A dog barked back in a show of support and I lay half awake under this combined barrage.

The straw mattress bunched uncomfortably under my cramped muscles, so I shifted position, even as those tiny ambassadors of the new day played hide and seek with the rough contours of the dreary, mud-brick walls. Then the exasperating intruders had the effrontery to shine on my face. I pulled the coarse cover high up over my cheeks and instantly sneezed. My eyes opened fractionally then blinked shut, dazzled by the light. I turned over in frustration and buried my head deep under the pillow. This strategy didn't work, for, presently, unimportant but niggling thoughts of the day ahead flitted through my mind, and I sighed and stretched my limbs like a cat does when it's disturbed. It was time to wake up.

The last of the deep shadows fled before the strengthening blush of the newborn morning as I sat bunched against the wall, listening to a divine song created by innumerable birds that burst like a refreshing shower into the small room. As I quietly meditated, random plans took shape and became concrete in my mind. Then, filled with an unusual sense of purpose, I swung my feet to the ground, meeting the familiar cold of the packed earth with warm flesh.

I slipped off the thin tunic and splashed water from a nearby bucket over myself, shuddering as the icy water touched bare skin. The discarded clothes felt cool to the touch, so I hurriedly pulled them back on. I huddled into the fabric, shivering like a wet dog, until at last I finally warmed up.

"If only Benjamin was here with me now; he would walk me to the temple," I murmured longingly, twisting up my long hair.

I sighed as I dipped a cracked cup into the water. Then I grabbed yesterday's left-over crust of dry barley bread and sat down on the rumpled bedding to munch the meagre breakfast—a small comfort swiftly overshadowed by my endless longing.

Nothing in life, I reflected pensively, had prepared me for the challenge that *that* voice declared so convincingly above the multitude. His words played over and over in my mind like a hungry bird circling for prey. They were as confronting now as when I'd only just heard them. How can such simple statements be so life giving?

Everything's different now, and even I have changed, I mused, flicking off a few crumbs. Then I stretched across the platform and picked up a tiny clay pot. I idly fingered the pattern as my thoughts turned dreamily back to Benjamin. He was so gentle, yet on occasion he could be very firm. I smiled, remembering. Benjamin would want to follow that man around the country-side ... with or without me. *But that's not my style; I'm too much like a settled tortoise.* In my mind's eye I saw Ben's eyes glint in agreement. Blinking rapidly, I smeared back the tears with my free hand. To distract myself, I considered the pot I was holding. It possessed the last thing I valued. Abruptly, I turned it over and emptied the scanty contents into a damp palm and then slipped over to grab my cloak, stumbling over the water bucket as I went.

Now there was water everywhere! The thirsty soil rapidly drank up the splash, leaving behind only a wet mark the size and shape of a giant teardrop. Somehow the tear was cheering, as if even our belongings missed him! This was one of those rare moments in life where something so simple as an accidental spill can seriously damage the isolating walls of loneliness built over a lifetime.

Wrapped in the warm folds of the cloak, I stepped quickly and determinedly out into the nippy cool of the crisp and frosty morning. I hurried along, gulping in the icy air. *I'll need to keep this speed up if I want to make it to the temple and back again before the cobblestones warm up and burn the soles of my feet,* I decided, marvelling afresh at the sharp contrast between the cold spring mornings and the burning hot afternoons.

Random flea-bitten dogs scurried to unknown destinations in search of adventure as the narrow, empty streets gradually filled with the huddled bodies of men and women leading their livestock to where the gates opened onto the grassy slopes beyond. I smiled sadly. Until recently, this had been our custom as well, but difficult times required me to sell the last of our goats. Benjamin's expressions were captured and mirrored in the pleasant, homely faces of those passing by. I shivered again. How could so much change in only a few short months?

The low, mist-wreathed vermillion sun discarded its veiled rosiness as it slowly ascended, as if abandoning too warm a scarf, revealing a light, bright violet-blue. The high-pitched cries of children bounced off the walls as they spilled out of too crowded homes to chase one another down the cramped alleys. Their boisterous fun was infectious and I laughed.

Suddenly, something hard rammed into me from behind. I yelped even as I toppled over and fell—sending the precious treasure from one hand high into the air—arms and legs spread-eagled ungracefully. Pain stung my palms as I hit dirt, and the rough edges of the cobblestones tore into exposed skin. I lay dazed for a moment, then crawled to my knees and lifted my head to stare straight into the round, concerned eyes of an imp.

"Sorry, didn't see you. Are you hurt?" he panted, the words pouring rapidly in high, bubbling notes from a small, pink mouth.

"No, I'm fine," I assured him, touched by this unexpected thoughtfulness. Flexing my limbs gently, I shifted onto my heels and grinned ruefully. Anxiety faded and the freckled, grubby face split wide open in return. He bent down and retrieved the scattered coins.

"Here's your money."

"Thank you," I said, grabbing the two coins somewhat possessively from his grimy little fingers, even as other curious children crowded about.

I stood slowly; intensely aware of alert, inquisitive eyes watching my every move. I carefully inspected my hands and clothes before brushing the dirt off. When it became apparent to all that no bones were broken they began to disperse, disappointed.

An older youth leading the pack turned and hollered for the young boy to follow and, after hesitating a moment, he spun around and fled. I stared at the back of the retreating lad, feeling sad. We had no children, Benjamin and I, but that didn't matter to me so long as he was with me. Then one morning, suddenly and unexpectedly, he'd taken ill. He'd been sick before, but this time was different. I was so afraid. I'd begged God to keep him alive, but it seemed as though He were deaf to all pleas, and soon I was left shedding bitter tears through long and empty nights.

I walked slowly on, caught up again in that awful moment, feeling once again the intense loss. Friends assured me that Benjamin was with God; that he was in a better place. Their kindness hadn't made it any less painful or less lonely. Seeds of bitterness sprouted, choking those well-intentioned words of comfort much like a python slowly squeezing the life from its defenseless victim until I, too, wanted to die. Then one afternoon some months later, I stumbled across a multitude gathered around a man standing on a hillside. His words drifted over the crowd.

"Blessed are you who are poor, for yours is the kingdom of God. Blessed are you who hunger now, for you will be filled. Blessed are you who weep now, for you will laugh."

"Laugh! That's a joke!" I'd cried, shaken by the sheer audacity of the words.

No-one would ever call my pitiful state "blessed" unless he was mad, and I scoffed at those contradictory phrases. What I wasn't prepared for was their power and persistence. It seemed impossible to forget them, and I was angry with those statements. The words played over and over again in my mind all that evening, and even as I'd tossed and turned on the mat that night, they robbed me of sleep, like water tumbling consistently, surely, when the snow melts, turning a trickling creek into an unstoppable river.

Imagine laughing again, imagine no more tears .... but was that really possible? Then, along with the multitudes, I too sought out the Galilean before he and his disciples moved on, feeding greedily on every word. The inspiring affirmation poured life-giving oil on the raw and open wounds in my heart until all the suffocating weeds of resentment withered away.

"Oh, how good God is that He forgives and heals and fills us with such a glorious hope!" I said, addressing no-one in particular. I almost skipped along the road like a child in anticipation of a treat.

The imposing structure of the temple glimmered in the mid-morning sunlight. Light and shade wove an intricate dance together across the beautiful cream coloured stones interlaced with marble and gold. I slipped quickly through the culturally diverse and jostling throng that steadily marched towards the arched entrance. An occasional greeting rang out above the general hum as individuals recognized one another, but no-one addressed me, and I spoke to none. It began to feel odd to be alone. My fast pace gradually slowed and, on reaching the wide, shallow steps fronting the impressive building, my feet finally faltered. The last time I came here Benjamin was with me. How safe I'd felt with him. Was I really brave enough to face entering alone? A shrill screech close by made me jump, and my eyes shut involuntarily.

"Don't be such a goose," I rebuked myself angrily. "It's only a silly bird!"

Gathering nerve, I passed through the archway that led into the Great Courtyard and gazed apprehensively about. The stalls of a thriving market lined the walls of the court and hummed with busy activity. Money-changers stood by their tables under shaded porticoes. Voices bargaining for the best prices mingled with the bellowing of pitiful, caged animals. Amid the din, a zealous teacher of the law struggled to hold the interest of a few students, while the rest of them cast bored eyes about, hopeful of a distraction.

A Pharisee in a splendid, blue-fringed robe picked his way carefully through the throng, pausing only to loudly applaud contemporaries. His manner reeked of affectation, and I felt small beside these prominent men. I moved away towards the Woman's Court, which was situated in the Jewish quarters beyond the walls of the great courtyard. Before long, out of the corner of my eye, I noticed the Pharisee head in that same direction. Behind me a murmur rippled through the crowd as yet another celebrant was noted. The temple at that moment felt less like a sanctuary than ever before.

I clung to my shabby cloak; the rough wool felt like the warm embrace of a friend against my trembling skin. I consoled myself that it wouldn't be long now. The Pharisee was now directly ahead, and I backed up a little. He stopped just short of the entrance to converse with a friend, and I slipped by unnoticed.

All of the sudden, a prosperous merchant, accompanied by a string of servants, swept me out of the way as though I were an insignificant gnat. They marched on through the wide open doors, their bountiful gifts teasing my reeling senses with the aromatic scents of fresh mint, dill, cumin, and the exquisite, musky notes of nard.

Feeling like a newborn duckling staring doubtfully at turbulent wind-tossed waves, I hovered before the gaping doors in an agony of indecision. Finally, I stepped tentatively into the dim interior, my eyes adjusting slowly to the muted light.

Directly in front of me stood a young but distant relative of Ben's, engrossed in thoughts of his own. I squirmed uncomfortably; I hadn't seen him since the funeral. Perhaps I could slip away before he noticed me to save us both from an awkward reunion. It was a mistake to have come!

Just then the Pharisee brushed past. "Good day to you, young man! I see your brows knit in troubled thought. Is there a prayer I may say on your behalf?" he cried.

My cousin raised anguished eyes. "Perhaps ... if you can answer this question. Why would God require a man to sell all his riches and give to the poor in order to be perfect?"

This was my chance to flee. I turned and looked straight into the thoughtful eyes of a vaguely familiar man standing with a group of men. Troubled, I swung round again and stared instead into the startled, disapproving eyes of the Pharisee.

He pointed at me, his shrill voice ringing with shock as he said, "God does not require that or we would all be reduced to the contemptible state of that poor creature over there—a weed on the landscape of life, forgotten even as it's noticed."

I stood rooted to the ground, icy cold and then unbearably hot, registering the quick intakes of breath, feeling the stare of shocked eyes. My empty stomach chose that moment to loudly growl its discontent. I hung my burning head. My clothes felt restrictive, stifling even as sweat pricked my skin. My stomach began to contract and I tasted bile.

Another wave of cold, followed rapidly by heat, swept over me, increasing the sensation of nausea. I swallowed hard. The world about me turned a hazy grey and then began to spin. I reached out a clammy hand groggily and grasped nothing but air. I gawked dizzily at the swirling nothingness, until—at last—it spun sickeningly, drunkenly like the ending turns of a toppling plate. All at once the gray vacuum vanished, much like the erased strokes of a graphite pencil, and the colours and shapes normalized again. The sharp edges of the two tiny coins cut like cat's claws into the lacerated, blood-dried skin. The pain seared my numbed brain, and I unlocked my clenched hand. I stared at the two minute and contemptible coins. Suddenly their battered and worn dullness reminded me forcefully of tiny winter-blown leaves curling at the edges—good for nothing!

Hot blood rushed back into my face; *they* were the reason I was here!

Quickly, like a drowning man clinging with all his might to a flimsy piece of driftwood, I scrunched up trembling fingers to hide the coins' repulsive smallness. Was I so foolish as to think this could mean anything to God?

The negative thought was instantly challenged by another—the words so clear and persistent that I almost glanced up to see if someone spoke them.

"Blessed are you who are poor, for yours is the kingdom of God."

The words resonated over and over in my mind like ripples of waves brushing the sand gently across a water-swept shore-line. Then my tense fingers slowly loosened their grip like the petals on a budded flower to reveal the two minuscule but priceless coins nestling in the centre of my hand, for now they held all the wealth of my thankful heart.

It was eerily quiet in the room. Deliberately keeping my head averted from the two men directly in front of me, I sought and found the nearest treasury chest. Even though it was only a few feet away, the distance felt more like a mile!

I stared agonizingly at the box, willing it to come to me.

"Blessed are you who are poor ..." The words had taken on a life of their own, strengthening my flesh. My feet slid submissively forward as though obeying a higher command. Soon I was beside the open chest, the coins rolling down and off their dirt-scratched bed to join the gleaming pile of gold.

I didn't care that the few clinks resonating so loudly in that silent room revealed, undeniably, to all listening ears how pitifully small the offering really was. I had done what I set out to do. The mission was accomplished! I turned to leave and caught again the gaze of those attentive eyes. Then, as he addressed all those about him in a voice rich with joy, I realized who he was!

"I tell you the truth; this poor widow has put in more than all the others. All these people gave out of their wealth, but she out of her poverty put in all she had to live on."

Destitute

The heavy rain eased and the autumn sun shone bravely through the lingering leaves to salute the funeral procession moving slowly down the tree-lined avenue. A glorious profusion of rust red, burnt orange, and golden-brown leaves, like pebbles dipped in water, lay matted in a carpet below the firm, stick-like arms. It was still—unearthly still. Not a whisper of wind rustled the hushed trees. It was as though nature were bowing her head to pay tribute to the body of the big-hearted old woman being borne along on the bier.

The leaf-strewn pathway ended in a small field with a grassy mound at its far end. The cortege continued like a troop of elephants ... slowly, silently across the clearing to the base of the latter and then halted. Here, the men bearing the load gently set down their burden. One man moved slightly apart from the tightly-knit crowd that clustered together. He was tall and well built with thick black hair and beard and piercing, dark grey eyes. He stepped closer to the corpse and gently loosened the cotton cloth that covered the face, placing it tenderly upon the linen strips dressing the body. His expression was pensive, but not overly sad, as he gazed down at the placid, waxen face with its sweet smile still lingering on frozen lips. The tears had come and gone and now a deep, profound, and unshakeable peace was upon him, lightening his face. Every now and then a look, almost of puzzled awe, was thrown his way from first one and then another of the crowd.

At a nod of his head, three men with shovels stepped wordlessly forward and began attacking the soft, sodden ground with repetitive strokes, lifting and tossing the soil effortlessly over their shoulders. The digging commenced rapidly, and a long shallow pit began to take shape. Now and again a digger would pause and wipe the sweat off his brow. Still, no words were uttered, and the crowd glanced furtively back and forth from the silent diggers to the tall serene man. The silence unnerved them, and they shifted uneasily. Soon the burial order would be given and then they would be free to leave this unnaturally quiet ceremony. But the man was oblivious to their obvious discomfort; his face was the face of a man buried in the distant past—a past almost perfect for its smooth years of pleasant memories if it were not for the overly warm spring, the first of three that swelled into a blistering summer and birthed death over the land, so that even the grasshoppers dragged along the ground. Nothing had shaped and defined his existence more than the memorable events that came in the wake of *that* first spring.

The day that marked the beginning of these occurrences was hot— hotter and drier than any other of his young life. The man shut his eyes, aware of every detail as if it were just happening. The air felt fixed, as though forever holding its breath. The heat of the sun beat down mercilessly on the tired looking barley bravely trying to survive under its piercing glare. He was running along the paths that bordered the sun-baked fields to meet his mother, watching the puffs of dust as they rose and fell in defeat under each conquering stride. He felt so alive, so childishly invincible in his ability to triumph over any and all that life could throw his way. His interest was caught by the sight of a large scarab clumsily rolling a ball over a small mound of sand. He stopped to look at it. It was in that moment, while watching the insect's frustrated efforts to prevent the ball from trundling backwards, that he noticed his mother's unusually drooping figure. Something about her sagging figure, merging so well with the wilting barley, was disturbing. Then she saw him and straightened and smiled, but this did little to ease the bewildering impression.

The brutal sun held its blockade on the heavens, and soon the desperate community began sacrificing cattle in an attempt to appease the gods. The smoke from the many fires touched the ends of the sky. There was a strange appeal in the feverish festivities—one that drew him irresistibly. The fierce fires roared and leapt on past dusk, their savage blaze birthing an unconstrained fire within, and later that evening his mother found him dancing wildly with the neighborhood kids.

"I know this is fun, but these celebrations can get out of hand," she cried, stopping him. "The gods can be very fickle and demanding and, sometimes, when the rain does not come and the famine is severe, it's not just the cattle that are sacrificed. I couldn't bear it if anything were to happen to you; you are all I have in this world. Let our neighbors do as they please without us. Anyway, I'm not convinced that the statues we worship are truly gods; not one of them has ever answered any prayer of mine."

"They must be gods!" he shouted, stunned. He'd never heard such views expressed before. He just assumed that she believed the same as everyone else.

She stared at him for a moment, and then said: "Perhaps they are, but they don't seem real to me. Besides, I don't have anything to offer for my sins. Even if I did, their response is unpredictable. It's hard to please the gods."

"You haven't done wrong!" he challenged, but she only smiled sadly.

"It's almost impossible to do no wrong."

"I've been bad, too; the gods must be angry with me, too."

"You're too young to worry your head about such things," she gently reprimanded. "Anyway, the only god that I've ever heard of to actually intervene in the lives of men is not one of our gods, but the god of the Jews, and only they have access to him."

The man, caught up in the unfolding drama, grinned wryly. They had no idea then that this was a conversation they were not going to get away with.

The harvest came and went, and little was gleaned from that blackened tangle of ruined stalks. Although food was scarce, his mother never turned away any who came begging. He never thought to question her generosity; it was so much a part of her. The man's stomach churned as he thought of the hunger. That awful, constant hunger! Sometimes the hours between the meagre rations were agonizing, and it felt as though a belt was tightening around his belly until it hurt so hard he wanted to cry.

By the summer's end he became so weak that all he felt like doing was sleeping. The days blurred together, and at times he would open his eyes to see his mother's worried face looking down at him. Then she would stroke his hair and say something comforting, but each time she grew more distant, even as the dreams felt more real, tugging him away from her and into fun-filled moments that lasted longer and longer—moments where even food smelt and tasted so real, like on that exceptional day he smelt the bread! Yummy, yummy bread!

"Son, the most amazing thing has happened! You must wake up; you cannot die now! Not now!"

"What is it? What's the matter?" he mumbled drowsily, feebly pushing away the hand disturbing the dreamy, delicious smells.

"Wake up and look at this bread; *it's a miracle!* Oh, please *wake up and taste it!*"

He struggled to rouse himself, not sure where reality lay. He glanced groggily over at the bread she held in her hand. It looked and smelt real enough. He sipped the water she offered him and stared disbelievingly at the loaf; it was so big!

"Eat a little, son; the bread really is real!"

He bit greedily into the bread, biting his sunken cheek hard.

"Slow down, son; eat slowly. Just a little for now. You can have more later," his mother cautioned.

After a few pitifully small mouthfuls, his shrunken tummy fully satisfied, he stared questioningly up at her.

"A stranger arrived today when I was near the well gathering sticks. He looked tired and asked for a drink of water, so I went to get it for him. Then he asked for bread. I told him I didn't have any, and that I was collecting wood to cook a last meal from the remaining handful of flour and little bit of leftover oil for the two of us to eat, before we both die! He said I was not to be afraid, that I was to go home and bake a small cake of bread and give it to him, for the god of Israel would ensure that there was some flour and oil left over—enough to make something for the two of us, until the rains came. Despite the evident sincerity, this was a new line, one that I hadn't heard before, and I smiled at the nerve of the man. On the way home I began thinking: *Why shouldn't he live? You and I are going to die anyway, even if the rains come.* I am already too weak to work a day in the fields, and it will be months before the crops are ready for gleaning. When I reached the house you were lying so peacefully. It seemed a pity to wake you, so I made a little loaf of bread and took it to him, thinking I would come back and die alongside you.

As I left, he reminded me to make something for ourselves, and ended up repeating his earlier words: "For this is what the Lord, the God of Israel, says: 'The jar of flour will not be used up and the jug of oil will not run dry until the day the Lord gives rain on the land.'" Suddenly I wasn't amused, but angry. Did he really think I was that gullible, that I would believe that his god *actually* spoke to him? Well, as soon as I reached the house, I looked in the jar of oil. Amazingly there was *still some left*! I rushed over to the pot of flour and there was some there too! I knew that I'd used the last of it to make that loaf for the stranger. For a while I couldn't stop looking in the containers at the flour and oil. Then, realizing I was wasting precious time, I baked this loaf using *all* the remaining flour and oil. While it was baking, I glanced again in the jars and the *same* amount of flour and oil was there, *just as if I hadn't used any at all!*"

"Who is he, Mom?" he cried.

"He says his name is Elijah!"

"His God *must* be the real one!"

The man's breathing quickened as he relived the rush of intense joy he'd felt as a boy at this discovery.

Nearby, a couple of people shuffled nervously, hoping to attract his attention and someone coughed loudly, clearing his throat. A young boy left the agitated assembly and pressed close against the man's side. Startled, he glanced down and then smiled and ruffled the mop of curly hair gently. He was much the same age when he met Elijah. Even now, he could see that fascinating face with its wild, white hair and long angular features with the jutting hawk-like nose as clearly as when he'd first stared shyly up at Elijah. The man's muscular frame, too, was impressive under the unfamiliar goat-skin garments, and when he spoke it was with a calm and indisputable authority, unlike other men.

The child clinging to the tall man felt uncomfortable under the silent, watchful gaze of so many eyes and tugged urgently on his father's arm, again disturbing the deep reverie. The man started guiltily as he caught sight of the gaping grave, and it brought him thoroughly back to the present. He bent and, with just the slightest wince, retied the linen wrap lovingly over the woman's face, forever hiding the pleasant, familiar features. This done, he gestured to the three men to lower the stiff body into the grave. The men, relieved to be employed again, hastily complied and then resumed their quiet shoveling. The man's arm tightened about the boy as the blanket of earth slowly enveloped the dear body, and again grief briefly troubled the tranquil features. An attractive woman moved closer and laid a reassuring hand upon his back. He smiled absently at her; his thoughts already back in that season of miracles.

Elijah was welcomed into their home as an honoured guest, and before long the stairway that led up to the prophet's lair on the rooftop held the same fatal attraction for him as a piece of cheese to a mouse, and, like a mouse, he would instantly vanish the moment Elijah's footsteps thudded on the stone landing above. A mouse is a good analogy, thought the man with some amusement, for it took him the best part of a month before he could muster up enough courage to ask Elijah the question that plagued him daily. Then, one day, almost by accident, it popped out.

"Elijah, why did your God send this drought?"

The man remained silent for a moment and then asked, "Boy, have you ever made a pot out of clay before?"

He nodded shyly.

"Then you know how proud you can feel when you look at your handiwork."

It was more of a statement than a question, but he nodded again.

"Well, how would you feel if you found the pot all scratched up and dirty? Wouldn't you be a little upset and try to fix it up? What if, no matter how hard you tried, you couldn't? Perhaps then you might be tempted to destroy it and start all over again. Is that right?"

Again he just nodded.

"That's how the God of Israel feels about us. In the beginning, God made man in his image and blessed him to rule over creation. God saw that what He had made was very good. Then man abandoned God's commands and sin entered his heart and, like the pot, he became marred. Although man's heart is evil from childhood, God is merciful and patient, and forgives all who repent and turn back to Him. But, when man resists God, he brings trouble such as war, disease, famine, and drought on the land. Then, when his heart turns back to God, he enjoys peace and prosperity for a time. Every honourable decision he makes, and then acts upon, undermines some of the negative impact evil thoughts have on his character, and in that moment he catches a glimpse of who God originally designed him to be, for he is more like God than he realizes. Think on what I have just said and perhaps you will begin to understand some of the God of Israel's ways."

He stared up in awe at Elijah, feeling a little lift of pleasure, for suddenly the God of Israel felt as approachable and real as the man standing before him, and as unlike their selfish gods as a living plant is from a lifeless stone.

The flour and oil continued miraculously to appear each day—never too much or too little! His mother always saw to Elijah's needs first, and then shared their portion with any and all who turned up hungry on the doorstep. After a while he grew so accustomed to the unusual event that it became commonplace. A smile touched the corners of the man's mouth; how he'd hero-worshipped Elijah, copying his pose and tone so identically that it often made his mother laugh. Then one day he developed a high temperature, and within a few hours his body succumbed to a raging fever.

"Please don't let him die, God of Elijah. Please don't take him away from me," his mother begged as he slipped in an out of dreamless sleep. "What do you have against me? Have you come to remind me of my sin and kill my son? Oh please don't take him away from me. Don't blame him for *my* sin. Please don't let him die; let him live!"

The effort of fighting the fever was too exhausting, and finally he let go. Unexpectedly, he found himself in a lush valley that stretched endlessly towards a brilliant, glowing horizon. Thick, vivid flowers perfumed the air with a rich and sweet scent where they edged verdant grassy borders. All around were happy sounds of gurgling laughter, which seemed to tumble out from the blossoms, and feeling more alive than ever, he dashed joyfully forward. The beautiful pulsating meadow grew brighter and brighter the farther he ran.

Then suddenly, jarringly, he found himself staring into Elijah's intense, pale eyes. Relief swept over the man's face as he bent and effortlessly picked him up and carried him downstairs, straight into his mother's outstretched arms.

"Now I know that you are a man of God and that the word of the Lord from your mouth *is* the truth," she cried excitedly.

The last sod of earth was smoothed into place and the crowd, free at last, hastily and noisily dispersed, ending his reverie. They respected the man and his dead mother; she had been good to many of them, but that which they couldn't understand made them suspicious and uncomfortable. This was an unusual funeral with none of the traditional hired mourners wailing before the gods.

The tall man wrapped his arms about his wife and son as he watched the community's rapid departure. Their response was to be expected; he knew that although as a family they were accepted, the locals did not consider him one of them, and he sighed deeply. Strangely, the sigh was not one of sorrow, but of anticipation, born from a longing to once again experience that place—the place where he knew, unquestionably, his mother was, and where someday he, too, would be.

Desperate Measures

*"The thief comes only to steal and kill and destroy,
I have come that they may have life; and have it to the full."*
—John 10:10

Trees lining the sandstone road cast smoky beige shadows across the bumpy surface, which thread its way like uneven stitches through flourishing fields of wheat and barley, the verdant greens and yellow golds blending well against a backdrop of clear blue sky. Here and there whitewashed houses sparkled like pearls amid this fertile quilt sloping gently down to the very edge of the sapphire Sea of Galilee. Nature determined with the aid of man to please the eye of the natural enthusiast, but all this effort was lost on the solitary trekker who, tottering drunkenly over to the nearest trunk, slumped like a jellyfish at its shady foot.

A couple of labourers, relaxing under deep shade nearby, paused their chatting to watch this strange behavior. They noted the ashen pallor and floppy weakness, and their immediate conclusion was that the traveller was suffering from too much heat. Then one of them casually stood up and lumbered over with an earthen jar full of cool water. This was gratefully accepted, and the weary traveller sipped greedily. A few brief words were exchanged before the man returned to his friend. Satisfied that this was all that was required, the two men soon forgot the stranger and resumed their low-toned discussion. Had they been more perceptive they might have paused to wonder why the new arrival's body still sagged and the face stayed sickly pale. They also might even have noticed the deeper shadows dressing the world-wary eyes and the down-turned, discouraged mouth, marring the wistful loveliness of countenance, all hinting at a more severe diagnosis.

The woman relaxed against the rough bark, weary to the bone, and grateful that she was a stranger to these workmen. If they knew, even suspected her problem, they would shun her like a leper. She would be forced to move on. But she was tired—deathly tired—of being forever on the march. She sighed; soon it would all be over ... and then what? Would there be the peace and the rest she craved, or would it be even worse?

Would God really fling her away like a dirty, soiled rag into the waterless pit, even as predicted so cruelly by those back home, to face alone the countless terrors lurking there? Her eyes dilated. This was the worst of it all; there was no certainty ... no knowing what lay behind that final breath. If only she could *know* for sure. It was this fear that had driven her for so long to keep risking rejection wherever she went in search of a cure. But the bleeding persisted, sapping all her youthful energy, her very lifeblood, insidiously dissolving even this last tenacious resolve. She was losing the battle to live, and she knew it. And now here she was, sitting alone, with only a tree to offer any protection or comfort. A single, solitary tear slid slowly down a thin and sallow cheek.

Twelve years ... it's a long time, she mused. *Was I ever young and carefree, or was it all just a dream, an illusion—a shadow with no real substance?*

Born advantaged, with every privilege wealth and position could offer, she had known nothing of suffering, of what it felt like to be an outcast. But all this can change in an instant, as she'd so painfully discovered. The devouring torment that troubled her daily began like a tiny blemish upon the idyllic canvass of her young life. At first there was much hope of a quick recovery, but when healer after healer failed to treat the perplexing condition, the shame and despair intensified. All her girlish dreams of being a wife and a mother disintegrated as a very different reality forged a new and lonely course. She soon became the butt of cruel jokes and unsolicited remarks as the neighborhood debated on what sins she and her family had committed to be so stricken by God. But even these rebuffs faded in comparison to the unbearable pain of being shunned. She could feel again the sidelong glances watching her every move, catch again the relief on their faces when she went the other way. Then there was the cleaning—the constant cleaning after her. Surreptitious at first and then blatant, violating her spirit, degrading her sense of self-worth, until she felt as worthless as a pile of horse manure. She had become untouchable!

· A soft laugh caught her attention, and she turned to watch the effortless antics of one of the men as he mimicked something amusing to his friend.

"How wonderful to have endless energy like that, to be filled with the sheer joy of living," she muttered enviously.

"*Why* do I keep thinking like this? Why can't I just accept the inevitable and give up and die?" she screamed inwardly, suddenly angry with herself, with the world about her, and with God ... mostly with God! She glanced away and shifted position so that her back was toward the men.

"Hope is such an odd thing," she reflected bitterly, tasting salt as the solitary tear trickled over the edge of her drooping lip. "It's been so long now, and yet I can't stop hoping for a miracle. Why do I hope so, when it will probably never happen? Because somehow, even after all these hard and fruitless years, I *still* don't believe I deserve this," she spat out, every muscle in her body suddenly tense and taut before weakly collapsing again like a new-born calf on its too fragile legs.

"I don't care that everyone back home thinks that I've committed some awful sin. I *know* it's not true! If I had done something bad that would be different, so *why* God ... *why* have you afflicted me? *Why* don't *you* vindicate me? What have I done that is so bad, so different, to make you reject me?" The habitual questions hovered unanswered in the air. Utterly vexed, she crushed a clump of grass, bruising the young, fresh blades.

She mulled over the problem while aimlessly, dejectedly, watching a bee chase away some ants collecting the nectar from a nearby flower, then busying itself at the same task. As usual, the overly familiar problem remained stubbornly unsolvable.

"Perhaps I *am* as bad as they say," she whispered sadly, finally acknowledging defeat.

Presently, the low drone of voices mingled with the gentle rustling of the leaves, producing a hypnotic effect. The soft, cooling breeze caressed away the furrows on her forehead, much like the soothing stroke of a mother's hand on the fevered brow of her child. Slowly and surely, she slipped into a deep and relaxing slumber.

The agreeable quiet was suddenly broken by a shrill, discordant voice demanding an audience.

"Hey, Luke! Josef! Can you hear me? It's me, Miriam. I'm coming over."

The traveller peered through sleep-heavy slits in the direction of the sudden disturbance, even as an older woman sprang into view.

"Yes, they and everyone else for miles around can hear you. Don't you realize that you are a menace to the peace?" she moaned drowsily before settling back into the welcome rest.

"Hi, you all. Has anyone heard how Jairus' twelve-year old is doing?" asked the woman, still shouting as she came nearer. "When I left a few days back she was very ill!"

The number *twelve* clamored annoyingly for admittance into the sleeper's conscious thought, and her eyelids fluttered. What *did* the woman say? Twelve was ill? No, that couldn't be it, only people were ill.

"Poor Jairus is beside himself with worry. No physician is able to cure her, and they say she's dying. You say the poor kid's only twelve? That's too young to die!" replied a patient but recognizable voice.

The traveller was suddenly wide awake. Not wanting to attract attention, she carefully straightened. Poor girl—only twelve years of age; why *that* was how long she'd been suffering!

"Jairus went down to the lake to beg the Nazarene to come and heal her. He said it's his only hope. If he succeeds in getting the man to come, they'll certainly pass this way." This information came from the other labourer.

"Well, if the rumours are true, then Jairus has nothing to worry about. The man is apparently Elijah, come back to life," broke in a clearly skeptical voice. "They say all he has to do is touch the sick and they are immediately well."

This had the instant effect of making the eaves-dropper forget her desire for obscurity; she twisted around to study the speaker. He was obscured from view, so she stretched forward in an effort to spot the puzzling originator of this incredulous statement. In doing so, she attracted the curious gaze of the farm labourer who'd earlier given her water. She squirmed guiltily and was about to turn away when she realized that he was no longer watching her. He was staring instead at the other woman who was gesturing wildly with her hands, apparently momentarily robbed of speech.

"There may be something to this prophet after all. Miriam is actually speechless," continued the unknown voice cynically. The eaves-dropper's lips twitched and she stretched cramped limbs as some of the tension drained away.

"That's what I came to tell you. That's only half of what he's done," cried the woman, finally managing to speak and ignoring the wisecrack. "I've just come from my nephew's funeral, except there wasn't one, because while they were carrying the lad out to be buried, the Nazarene named Jesus came up and stopped the procession. He took the dead boy's hand, commanded him to get up, and he *did!*"

The stranger gasped loudly but attracted no attention, the group as fascinated by this new information as she.

"No! But that's impossible!" said the man she'd met earlier.

"It happened, I tell you; I was there! Look, that must be them coming now!" yelled the woman excitedly, pointing down the road to a faint speck in the distance.

Why haven't I heard about him? she wondered, rising unsteadily. The sun was high in the sky, making the light almost a bright white, and she shielded her dull eyes as she squinted eagerly at the hazy horizon searching hard for some tell-tale signs of movement.

Who is this man? Can he really raise the dead just by touching them? What if he turns out to be a fake, just like the phony physician she'd last seen? Suddenly, she collapsed clumsily and grabbed the trunk for support, a painful spasm shooting through her chest at the brutal recollection of that visit.

Some men running a rag-tag donkey-train convinced her to travel with them to consult a hermit they'd spun a yarn about. She agreed, against her better judgment, and went with them. The trip took far longer than expected. Straddling the bumpy back of a bony and smelly donkey, while hot and dizzy and, not to mention, hungry for hours on end, was sheer torture. On arrival at what could not be called anything other than a hovel, the men were rough in their handling of her dismount. Before she'd fully regained her balance they rushed off to meet a thin, stooping figure just visible in the doorway of the ramshackle building. After conferring briefly with her, they disappeared into the cooler darkness beyond.

Appalled by this desertion, she hobbled painfully over to the woman, still waiting like a gaunt and predatory bird in the dense shadow, to enquire about the healer.

"He'll see you shortly. Wait under that cypress at the side of the barn until he comes over to treat you!" the woman rasped rudely as she pointed to an equally gaunt tree.

She stared with horror at the scrawny tree, and her heart tightened with pain. Here was no pleasant, welcoming shade offering a much need-ed respite, but a barely discernible silhouette created by the sun high up in the sky. Even the rickety shed offered little more than a thin sliver of shelter. "It's so hot! Can I at least have a drink of water?" she asked, her head-ache pounding in unison with each syllable.

The woman grunted something that sounded hopeful before dis-appearing into the cavernous darkness behind her. A burst of amused laughter broke the deathly quiet as she limped away. After an endless wait, during which time she gave up any hope of refreshment, the woman reap-peared carrying a small jar which she set down carelessly, slopping half the discolored water onto the thirsty ground. Although her thirst was great, she was barely able to drink the unpalatable liquid. Accustomed as she was to being ignored and ill-treated, each new occurrence dug a fresh wound.

When the unkempt hermit finally arrived, he brusquely demanded payment upfront, his breath reeking of wine. Not sure whether to comply, yet desperate for even the flimsiest chance of a cure, she paid the exorbi-tant fee. After a long and detailed history, he gave her a tiny jar of some putrid smelling potion that supposedly guaranteed a cure for not just her complaint, but every possible ailment. These overly profuse promises smacked of the quack and she realized that once again she'd been had. The tears came then, and also on that miserable ride back to town with her none too sober guides, at the utter wretchedness of everything.

She brushed away a stray hair that tickled her cheek in the slight breeze with a hand that visibly shook. This, she promised herself, was go-ing to be the very last time she risked again. Somewhere in that steadily approaching puff of dust was a man sent by God—a man they called Jesus. If he couldn't heal her, then no-one could!

A faint, almost musical, hum carried by gentle waves of wind touched her straining ears like soft petals brushing against skin. Expectation quiv-ered in the air, the very expanse vibrating new-born belief. The haunting fear began to weaken and lose some of its stranglehold over her mind as the muffled pulsating drumming of many feet gradually grew louder. Exuberant and unconstrained whoops of joy added their notes to the general symphony of sound like symbols clashing boldly and drew her, irresistibly, into a whirlpool of giddy anticipation. Enthralled, she watched the fluid mass loom larger and larger until finally, with a thunderous crescendo, it discharged into boisterous and identifiable individuality.

Could she dare to hope again? No, the question was more, could she dare not to. She would grasp at this last chance to defy death!

Faces were now easily distinguishable, and centre stage was a man in a white robe with an adoring crowd milling about him. She studied him with an unexpected pang of misgiving, even as the initial intense excitement cooled. The old questions crowded her mind. Would this Prophet be willing to help once he knew her story? What if those who condemned her were right and she was guilty and deserved to suffer? What if there was no pardon, no remission of sins? The thought of facing fresh exposure, so publically and before *this* man, crashed upon her like a thunderous wave, shipwrecking hope. She could not bear to read despising pity in his eyes, like that of all the other healers—not now, not after all the disgrace and humiliation she'd already endured.

She stared wildly around. Oh the absurdity of it all! Now that she'd finally found the *One* who could heal, she couldn't bear asking for healing. This was her last chance to resist that cruel destroyer of life, and if she aborted now, it was over –she was doomed!

"I have to ask, I *have* to. What else *can* I do?"

They were alarmingly near now, so near that the young children running ahead were now upon her … now ahead of her. This was the moment; he was almost abreast now. She tried to speak, but no words came. Her tongue felt thick, swollen, stuck; her hands icy, her head unbelievably dizzy. The world started spinning; was she going to faint? Oh no, not now! Fear tightened its ghastly hold as beads of sweat pricked her forehead. The moment came and went! He was passing by; the crowd was pressing in close, constantly touching and bumping him.

Touching him, bumping him… The thought was terrifying in all its implications, yet the possibility of wholeness was irresistible. Could she dare to do the same? According to the law, he would be defiled if she touched him, but who would know, *who could* know it was her? There were so many touching him; only God could know.

Only God!

For a moment she hesitated, daunted by the terrible possibility. It was a truly reckless thing to do, but what if that one touch healed her?

"It's madness to hope like this," she thought, mesmerized by the dangling blue tassels lining the edge of the prayer shawl draping his retreating back. The hope grew irresistibly, even as the panic settled. It was a risk not to ask publicly for healing but, if he was indeed from God as they said, why would she need to ask? The promise of healing was knotted into these tantalizing pomegranate shaped tassels, and this alone might be enough to heal. Oh to be whole again! She couldn't think about that; it was almost too much to imagine.

Why would she need to ask? Surely the power anointing him was for *all* the children of Abraham, even her.

Summoning her last remaining strength, she melted into the vibrant orchestra of life swirling about and pushed persistently through the crowd, not allowing her mind to think of anything except the man just ahead. She was close now—almost close enough to touch the edge of a tassel. Just one step closer and ... it was done! Immediately the bleeding stopped and she felt a burning heat, the fire of life, flowing through her—energizing, healing her.

"Who touched me?"

As a conductor with a single sweep of his hands brings an uncanny stillness, so his words brought a deathly quiet. For a few moments everything stopped—the excited cries, the shuffling of the crowd, the breathing of those close by, even her own heartbeat.

How can he know? She shivered as she stood shaken, thinking of that barely discernible pat while so many others had knocked against him. Only God could ...

Oh no, she thought, suddenly terribly afraid. *What will he do once he discovers the truth? I can't confess. I can't! Not here, not in front of this entire multitude.*

Those with him were addressing him. "Teacher, you see the people crowding against you, and yet you can ask, 'Who touched me?'"

Hope flickered momentarily; perhaps he would walk on and forget that slight touch. But Jesus kept looking around to see who it was. "Someone has touched me; I know that power has gone out from me." Standing before the powerful purity of the man, she suddenly understood clearly the sin now condemning her. It was exposed in all its ugliness. There was no mistake; she *was* guilty. Not of trying to cover over shameful rejection, but of robbing God! She had stolen His power and defiled this representative of God, and now her total self absorption was making her conceal the act like a common criminal. In that moment, she realized she did deserve to die.

"I have to be brave," she thought, convulsively shaking as a new and unfamiliar guilt tore up all argument to the contrary. Shutting her eyes tightly she fell at his feet. Her confession sounded utterly damning, even in her own ears, as she poured out the truth. Silence followed the outburst— chilling and terrible silence! The seconds crawled by slowly, painfully, as if they were hours instead of short ticks of time. The very air hung still, as if holding its breath, waiting for the inevitable recrimination.

The expected rebuke never came; instead, a strong, encouraging voice reached out across the space between them and gently lifted the awful weight of guilt bearing down on her.

"Take heart, daughter, your faith has healed you. Go in peace and be freed from your suffering."

Her tightly stretched nerves registered the response, experiencing the full power of the words in the flesh, even before her mind could comprehend them.

Daughter? Did he really say daughter? Dumbfounded and with eyes now wide she looked wonderingly into rich wells of sombre love, even as the heartening words hit home.

"God *has* accepted me! He's healed me! I belong, I *really* belong!"

Liquid Gold

"To the faithful you show yourself faithful."
—2 Samuel 22:26a

D o you want to hear my story? Well, it will take some time, so settle down, make yourself comfortable, and sip a cup of steaming hot tea while I tell you …

The knocking was insistent rather than demanding, like the constant drip, drip of water, and only quit when I swung open the door. My mouth must have gaped a little when I saw who was standing on the other side. The man coughed noisily and then mumbled a few inaudible words, which I took as a greeting. I nodded an acknowledgement and stared curiously. Affluence was visible in every layer of clothing and in the glint of gold, yet it sat strangely incongruously on the lender's lean and stooped body. The overall impression was one of scruffy untidiness rather than the polish and elegance of a rich man of means. His face, on the other hand, was anything but casual. The features were harsh and accentuated, the austere eyes guarded. Those same watchful eyes were set a little too close to a large nose, lending a wolfish look to his narrow face that his present reserved expression in no way diminished.

"What can I do for you?" I asked stiffly as he met my stare with one of equal interest. Although my husband had numerous dealings with him in the past, our lives never really touched. I only knew him by reputation, and what I'd heard did not make me desire a closer acquaintance.

His reply was sombre, sepulchral. "I am sorry to hear that your husband has passed away. He was a good man."

"Thank-you," I said, fully concurring. Courtesy demanded that I be polite, so I suppressed a strong desire to end the unwelcome call and waited uneasily instead.

He made no answer, his feet shifting awkwardly on the rough hewn doorstep. Then his eyes slid away from mine, increasing that peculiar feeling of distrust, and I began to wonder what lay behind this unexpected visit. Even though the condolences were kind, they were unnecessary.

The silence stretched uncomfortably, and when he still made no answering remark, I thanked him again and began to shut the door. Then his hand shot out to prevent me. This behavior unnerved me, and I was suddenly thankful that our house was one of many crammed into the narrow street.

"Wait a moment," he broke in, his stern eyes glinting like sharpened iron. "There is something else I need to discuss with you."

I looked at him questioningly, even as I relaxed slightly, for I thought it was probably only about some minor debts that my husband had incurred. "If it's just a matter of settling a few small debts ..." I began pointedly.

At this he made a gargling sound as if to speak and then, instead, his wide mouth curved open with a sneering smile, revealing, for an instant, large yellow teeth before snapping shut. As my words faded away he straightened to his full height and stared keenly down at me, reminding me again forcefully of a large and hungry wolf. I backed a bit behind the door.

A full minute passed before he spoke; he chose his words carefully. "I do not think you are aware that your husband borrowed a large sum of money from me a couple of years ago." There was just enough emphasis on the word *large* to make my heart skip a beat, but his next words set it racing. "And that he pledged to pay it all back within seven years. Regrettably, he is no longer here to make payment, and the remaining money is now due."

"Of course we'll pay whatever we owe as soon as possible," I said much too confidently.

A look of disdain crossed his face before his eyes slowly winked shut, rather like a dog does when you eyeball it, and I coloured uncomfortably.

"I don't think you understand," he added icily. "I repeat ... the outstanding sum is due *immediately*."

Then I faced the hard look in his eyes with a bravado I was far from feeling, for my toes had begun to tingle as they always do when I'm in some sort of trouble. There was another rather awkward pause before I managed to ask, "Just how large is the loan?"

At this he bent his head and fumbled for a moment within his cloak. Then he withdrew a papyrus scroll and with a small flourish handed it to me. I held the document as though it were lit on fire, my eyes never leaving his face. His glance slid meaningfully down to the scroll clutched limply in my hands, and I got the message. I unravelled and smoothed the parchment, and then with difficulty tried to decipher the squiggles that made up the script. Needless to say, I was unsuccessful. At last, with a disgusted sigh, he removed the deed from my unresisting fingers and began, slowly and emphatically, to read the contents out loud.

"It can't be true!" I gasped, cutting him short.

The moneylender continued to watch me closely in that peculiar dog-like fashion before he painstakingly re-read the last sentence.

"It can't be true; my husband never mentioned such a large sum. It's almost a year's wages; it will take us forever to pay this back!" I snapped out, now in real distress.

He unconsciously stroked his beard. My response appeared to have pleased him, for he made a conscious effort to refrain from ... smiling! I shuddered. I suppressed a desire to howl, even as he shot me another calculated glance. The suspense was unbearable, and I could hardly stand it. Something in that intent look told me there was more—something even more disturbing than the debt!

He cleared his throat again, but it was a while before he spoke. Again the silence between us stretched before he said, still emphasizing each word slowly and plainly, "As I mentioned before, the balance is due immediately. There is a grace period of a month, after which, if the debt is not paid up, your two sons will be sold to me as payment."

I think I must have groaned at this bald statement, for the world I knew had suddenly gone quite mad! In the midst of the madness, however, some part of my brain still functioned clearly, for I remember thinking, quite rationally, that this was what the call was really about. It was about my sons! He wanted my sons! But in that moment this was too harrowing to think about.

It could not be true; none of this could be true! I thought desperately as I watched him lick his lips and begin to clear his un-cooperating throat for the third time. This was the only repetitive pattern in all the craziness of this interview, and somehow it steadied me. Before he could say anything further, I cried out: "You cannot, my husband would never ..."

At this he waved the roll of parchment back and forth between us like some vanquishing sword, each feeble movement increasing the sense of entrapment. A smirk stretched the thin lips into a grotesque line. For a split second, his face became immeasurably cruel, and then he crooned, "It's all recorded here!"

I recoiled in horror before the avenging scroll. It seemed incredible to me that something so flimsy could contain such an awful judgment.

He nodded approvingly, his face suddenly congenial, but his eyes hard as flint. "No sense in fighting a legally binding contract," he agreed. "Indeed, your husband was always an honourable customer and had, I'm sure, every intention of paying back the loan. Perhaps that is why he apparently did not disclose the matter to you." Looking back on that call and on all that passed between us, I realized that was the moment I most felt like a trapped animal.

Then he anticipated and parried the desperate plea forming in my mind and finished off by saying; "I regret that I am unable to extend the date for you to repay the money beyond that allotted by the pledge, as I have pressing concerns of my own."

At this, words failed me. Only the irrepressible tears sliding down my cheeks betrayed any emotion, for I was like the proverbial lamb, silent before the slaughter.

He turned to leave and then, having second thoughts, hesitated and said; "I realize that this news has come as a shock, and that this is rather short notice, but bad things happen to all of us that we aren't expecting." The words literally purred out and were in marked contrast to the constant and impatient shuffling of those gangly legs.

He waited just long enough to be sure I was reasonably calm before dropping his persuasive voice to a deceptively silky tone. "You need time to think ... to adjust ... so I will come back in a fortnight. On my return, you can let me know how you intend to make good the debt, and we will finalize the necessary arrangements." With a distinctly dismissive nod, he abruptly turned and left, but not before I noticed another betraying grin edging that mobile and pitiless mouth.

I slumped heavily against the door frame, feeling like a leaf clinging limply to a broken twig after a raging, shaking storm. It was unthinkable that we had so much debt and that my sons were the collateral. Nothing made sense anymore—least of all why God had allowed this, for only an ill wind could have blown such a frightening and formidable opponent to our door.

Life had always been a struggle, but I was content. My only expectations were to have a kind husband, a place I could call home, and some children to make it all worthwhile. My husband's death was a hard knock, and even though it was tough for us to make ends meet, I was grateful that the boys were still with me. Now it looked as though I was to be stripped of it all—our home split apart, and my sons left to the mercy of a cold-hearted man like this. What he would do to them I couldn't even begin to imagine. A door slammed shut in my mind at this thought, and I made no attempt to open it, for I was on the verge of hysteria.

At that point I noticed a neighbor peering pryingly out of a window directly opposite. I pretended not to see and moved quickly into the welcome sanctuary of the house. I am a pretty private person and prefer to keep my pain to myself. Unless the confidant is an intimate friend, it soon becomes local gossip.

There is usually something so heart-warming about a fire, but that day the blaze failed to ease the chill in me as I looked around the cozy, familiar room. Everything was neatly in place and looked much as it did when I came here as a young bride. Although sparse in furnishings, it was rich and full with memories, and that is something no amount of money can buy. Both boys were born in this room. My husband was so pleased when the first sign of his strength turned out to be a boy, that he started calling our baby "Uzi." Soon everyone, including me, was using the pet name which means *strong*, as you might guess. When our next child arrived, my husband shouted the words "another *son*" at the top of his lungs, and the amused neighbors from then on dubbed the newborn *Ben*. The two nick-names stuck, and Ben became Uzi's second shadow. Once, my husband and I had laughed to see Ben waddling as fast as his little legs would carry him in the supreme effort to keep up with his older brother. If only we could have had a few more years together, but how quickly things change. And yet some things don't change; Uzi is still Ben's hero.

Although never in excellent health, my husband's condition must have been much worse than he'd let on for him to borrow so much money! I tried to mesh this new information with what I could remember of his behavior the last couple of years before the events leading up to his sudden death. Suddenly some strange and puzzling incidents slotted perfectly into place, and I sank against the wall, aware of a deep and aching sadness. It was true. He had indeed borrowed more than he could comfortably afford. How wearisome the burden must have been, and the idea of our sons as slaves, slaves to that beastly man, must have been unbearable! How I wished he could have trusted me enough to share it.

Then another thought, equally unpalatable, hit me. How on earth was I going to tell the boys this bad news following so soon after the death of their father? At that moment, I was grateful that they were busy working hard in some neighboring fields.

Working hard! This realization really hit home, and I threw myself on the bed, sobbing until I could sob no more and sleep claimed me.

Later that day, the door swung open and my eldest son, soon to have his bar mitzvah, flung his large and lanky body triumphantly across the threshold. "I'm first!" he yelled. "Mom, wait 'till you hear what …" Arrested in mid-sentence he stopped and stared at me. His younger brother, following hard on his heels, slammed into him.

"Ouch! Uzi, why did you stop so suddenly?" he shouted angrily.

Uzi put a restraining hand on his arm, quieting him, and turned back to face me. "Mom, what's the matter, what's happened?" he asked quietly, tersely.

I said nothing, for I was incapable of thinking of anything beyond how much like his nick- name he was becoming—strong in mind, limb, and muscle.

Ben, realizing that something was wrong, looked curiously at me. Under their combined and anxious stares, I burst into tears. At this they rushed over and hugged me.

"Boys, the most dreadful thing happened today," I blurted between sobs. "A man, a creditor from town, came demanding payment for a large sum of money your father borrowed. He brought a document with him, signed by your father, stating the amount. It's an enormous figure, and we've no way of paying it back."

"Yes we will!" declared Uzi after a moment, using a deeper tone than usual and staring determinedly at me. "We *will* find a way of paying it back, even if it takes us forever."

I know I smiled at that point, for the newly acquired pitch made his voice sound surprisingly like his father's. "It's only a month before the note is due," was all I managed to say.

"Oh," he muttered, damped.

"But that's ... not all ... the bad news," I finally added, choking on the words.

Ben's arms tightened about me. Then he asked anxiously, "What else did he say?"

My voice was thick and unfamiliar even to my own ears as I said, "He says that if we don't pay in time, the two of you will be sold to him to cover the debt."

Uzi shifted uneasily as he looked at me. Then, after a short pause, he asked, "What does that mean, exactly?"

I felt tense all the way up into my head as I answered, still with that strangely tight and hoarse tone. "It means that he will come and take you both away, and you will be his slaves until the debt is paid back in full."

The boys stared in horror at me. I could sense that they were having the same struggle I was having believing these words.

"Can he really do this?" Uzi demanded. "Can he really come and take us away from you and make us his slaves?"

"Yes," I replied, holding his gaze and noting the colour of his eyes change from grey to almost black. "Legally he can if we do not pay back this debt, and it might be many years before I see you again." I plunked heavily onto the rocker as my legs gave way. There was a short unhappy silence as the three of us stared hopelessly at each other.

Uzi was the first one to break the quiet, a premature crease created unfamiliar lines between his thick brows, as he worried out loud. "What will you do, Mom? How will you survive without us here to help you?"

"I'll manage somehow," I barely managed to say, touched to the core. "I just can't bear the thought of losing you both."

Ben's small face crumpled and his voice trembled as he said, "He must be a cruel man to take us away from you, Mom."

His brother quickly left my side and went to comfort him. "I won't let him separate us from Mom. We'll find a way somehow to pay that debt," he assured him.

"We don't have a lot of time," I tiredly reminded them, my heart torn between a mixture of motherly approval and despair at this awkward and sweet display of affection.

Then Uzi turned to me, his eyes very determined. "We'll just have to *make* him give us more time," he insisted.

"Well, we'll have to see what we can do before he returns," I answered, feeling weary to the bone. We were all battling to accept the news, and there was no point in further argument. I rose slowly to my feet, for it was almost suppertime, and then, assuming a false briskness, I said: "But in the meantime, I want wood chopped for the fire."

This request galvanized Uzi into action. With a look of relief, he covered the short distance to the door in no time at all, calling Ben over his shoulder to join him as he left to grab the ax. Then my youngest, after a last, quick swipe across the eyes, followed him out the door. Alone again, I sank back onto the rocker, my spirit profoundly disturbed. God, at that moment, felt very far away.

Supper that evening was a subdued affair. A quietness going against their nature presided heavily upon each boy. Intense feelings were building under the tension of unarticulated questions, but I didn't know if I was up to the storm I could feel brewing. Eventually Uzi, after gloomily contemplating his empty bowl for some moments, spoke up. "Mom, why did God take Dad when he knew we couldn't pay the debt without him?"

"I don't know, son," I replied with a sinking heart, sensing the underlying animosity as I watched the spoonful of soup hover in front of his mouth. He continued to look at me in a demanding way, and I tensed under this unuttered pressure to qualify my brief answer.

"But what I do know," I finally said, "is that your father was a good man; he believed in God and dedicated his whole life to serving him. I know that he is with God now. I realize this is not the answer you are wanting, but it's the truth." Unfortunately, my words came out more sharply than I had intended.

"So," cried the lad angrily, letting loose the hovering tempest I was dreading, "it *must* be God's fault that we are in this mess, because He could just as easily have kept Dad alive."

"Yes, in a way that's true," I replied, deliberately stretching the words out to calm all our churning feelings. Above all else, I did not want to be drawn into an emotionally charged argument. We were facing one of those tornado moments in life that can utterly destroy a family, and no matter what else hit us, I did not want their trust in God forever shattered.

"The prophets constantly warn us to remain faithful and not to turn away from trusting in God," I began mildly, but then ended rather emphatically. "We can't stop believing in God just because life takes a turn for the worse!"

Neither boy responded; Ben's face resembled uncooked pastry, while Uzi looked downright angry.

"It's easy to blame God, but harder to stand square and face with faith the punches life throws us," I rationalized, faltering a little, for these were brave words indeed and ones I wasn't sure I could live up to.

This temporarily calmed the emotional storm within Uzi, so I pressed stubbornly on, gaining courage from both boys' silence. "Circumstances don't dictate or control our faith; only we have that right! Difficult times can bring out the best or worst in us, and it is during these times that what we actually think and believe becomes clear, whether we really believe in God or will turn away in doubt."

I could see that I had their full attention now, so I switched tactics. "Perhaps the question should rather be, has Dad's untimely death, and the bad situation that we now find ourselves in, destroyed our belief in God?"

The concern uppermost in my mind was now expressed, and I waited nervously for a response while nibbling on the rye-bread. Brows were knit in deep thought while the two boys considered the problem from this new angle.

Ben finally broke the silence and said, "I don't think it has. I still believe in God, even if I don't understand." His brother looked at him in exasperated amazement.

"But it could have," I interjected before Uzi could respond. "Even as what is facing us can, if we allow it." Even as I felt the relief at Ben's reaffirmation of faith, I bristled as my eldest son's features set into the familiar mulish expression that usually spelt trouble.

"You may still believe in Him, but do you still *trust* him?" Uzi demanded of his brother. He turned to me and blurted on, the volume increasing with the strength of feeling expressed, "Surely if we trust Him He has a responsibility to take care of us, to rescue us from this mess?"

There was a short pause as both boys turned and faced me. If the truth be told, I was floundering with the same problem Uzi was wrestling with, and the sudden insecurity made me defensive.

"Do you think it's fair to expect Him to rescue us from a problem we have created?" I snapped, clinging to the only understanding I had. The look in Uzi's eyes became even more defiant.

He glanced sidelong at Ben and then back to me as he cried bitterly, "We may have made a mess of things, but He made the problem bigger by taking Dad from us."

At this, Ben squirmed about on his seat and, attracted by the shuffling, I peered at him. He appeared to be all eyes as his white, pinched face stared from Uzi to me, and I immediately switched back into parental mode. "We cannot dictate to God what He should or shouldn't do," I said, striving hard to be calm. "However, I do know that He will never leave us, and that He will help each of us get through whatever difficulty we have to face." This sounded good to me, so I warmed to the theme. "As I said before, most of my experience has been that He allows us to go through some pretty tough times, but that He protects us in the midst of them, if we still choose to love Him no matter how we might feel or what we might have to suffer."

An intensity of conflicting emotion shifted across Uzi's mobile young features as he thought through my answer. Then he retorted with passionate indignation, "I see what you are saying, but it doesn't answer the question; it simply lets Him off the hook! If God is responsible for us, then He is responsible for our messes, too. If He isn't responsible for us, how then can we trust Him?"

This answer floored me, and I kept silent.

And then a small voice across the table piped up. "Why did God make us so poor?"

I felt utterly unequal to answering this, and something deep inside cracked as everything inside me screamed the same question.

Ben hesitated a moment and then bravely continued. "Is it because He can't trust us with money?" he asked, his confused and hurting eyes holding my gaze steadily.

"Not at all," I finally managed, sounding as confident as I could, for this could not go unanswered. But if the truth is told, I was barely hanging onto the shreds of my faith. "God could easily have chosen to make us prosperous and given us much more than we deserve, but perhaps our trust at this moment would be in that wealth and not really centered in Him? Material comfort and possessions can be a much harder test to overcome, for it is hard not to become focused on money, like the lender who came around to-day. It is much better to be poor and generous than rich and greedy."

This seemed to comfort Ben, so I carried on. "This is our opportunity to discover just how strong our faith in God really is. My hope is that our belief in God remains strong in spite of every ..."

At that moment Uzi cut in, short-circuiting my justification of God, his mind still tracking with the earlier problem. "Mom, you said yourself that Dad served God faithfully. Dad also took care of us and God removed that responsibility from him. Now God, by default, is our only father, so we are His responsibility!" he exclaimed, looking exultantly from me to Ben.

Ben's expressive face assumed a dog-like devotion as he eyed his brother. "Dad said that God always hears us when we pray to Him," he butted in eagerly. "Just before Dad died, he told me to never stop believing in God, to trust Him no matter what happened. God will do something!"

Uzi turned to me. His eyes were alight with a sudden, wild hope. "Mom, think of all the miracles Dad kept telling us about. God can do anything!"

"Yes, He's in charge now," I agreed half-heartedly. But my consent came more from a desire to keep the peace than from any position of faith.

The boys were tired out from these emotionally charged events following a day of hard manual labor, so shortly after supper they said goodnight and were soon sleeping the deep and undisturbed sleep of youth.

I felt a touch of envy as I stood gazing upon their slumber that evening, for I longed to fly off into the elusive world of dreamland. That escape hatch, for the moment at least, remained firmly barred. I remember thinking how trusting they were and how unfair life was that innocent children had to suffer the consequences of the rules of an adult world. Then I prayed fervently for their faith not to be destroyed, for they were only children and did not fully understand yet how harsh life could be and what all this really meant for our family. And I totally missed the irony of this prayer.

There have been times in the past when I felt vulnerable and alone, but never to the degree that I felt in that moment. I moved over to where the rocker stood illuminated by the moonlight and sat down. For a long time I just sat and stared vacantly out the window at the deep shadows cast by the neighboring buildings under the starry night sky, thinking about how much I was going to miss the boys.

I had no idea how to even begin to clear the debt. There was not much equity in the house, and we had very little money. Even if we sold our home, we would only create a new problem, for now we would be in debt and homeless. Every idea I came up with fell horribly short of the sum needed, and my head felt as though it was fixed in an invisible vice with endless circular reasoning ending inevitably in a permanent dead-lock.

Finally, worn-out with worry, robbed of all sleep and at a complete loss as to what to do, I walked over to the food closet. In a fit of frustration I opened wide the doors displaying the meagre contents in the dim light to full advantage. Fresh tears trickled down as I lifted up the almost empty jar of oil and gazed despairingly at the remaining dark liquid.

Then I fell to my knees on the mat in the renewed strength of anguished despair.

"God, please help us. You are all I have to turn to. Oh God, please help us. Lord, they're good boys. Please don't let that brute take my sons away from me; oh please, don't let him! They're all I have now!" I pleaded over and over until even these desperate petitions petered away. I don't know how long I remained in the numb chambers of exhaustion before tiny strands of memory crystallized around a curious incident.

Our group of prophets had settled in Jericho a few years back. Then the men from the city had approached Elisha because the water was tainted and undrinkable. He'd taken a new bowl with some salt and thrown these into the spring, and immediately it became drinkable. Even as this incident played on the strings of recollection, a citation from King Solomon that my husband used to quote came back to haunt me: "You will keep your covenant of love with your servants who continue wholeheartedly in your way." Suddenly, understanding came. The reason why God healed the water was because the prophets moved here and this became their home. God is committed to caring for the needs of his servants and my husband was one of them! And now that I was in debt, it was God's problem. These thoughts merged into an idea and I shouted out loud: "That's it! Uzi is right! God is responsible for us. And now I must find Elisha!"

Peace came, easing my troubled mind, for as incredible as it sounded, it was true! He would take care of us! God was indeed answering me.

The air hung sweetly in layers of rich scent near the wild lavender bushes that following morning. Dusty coloured birds clung to thin branches and trilled musically, blithely unconscious of any who were heavy-hearted. Their feathery breasts swelled with pride, their sweet song calling all to bask in the freshness of the dewy morning. This wonderful evidence of a perceptive and imaginative hand behind the created order of things touched me, even though my mind was fixed on one goal only—to find Elisha and to find him as quickly as possible.

The area where the prophets prefer to hang out in our town is easy to find, and I eagerly scanned the walkways. They were busy with scurrying townsfolk but deserted by that select group of seers. They appeared to be hiding, and I wondered whether they were all cloistered in some remote spot with Elisha. I knew it was his custom to move between the three towns that housed the companies of prophets and that he might not be coming to ours for a while yet. It was imperative that I discover where he was so that I could plan how to intercept him. A fear that they might have gone on some lengthy pilgrimage bugged me, and I determined that, no matter what, I would find him—even if it meant journeying somewhere distant.

There aren't too many places to search, and I was just on the point of retracing my steps when I spotted an old associate of my husband's hurrying down a side alley.

"Do you know where I can find Elisha?" I called out.

"I have just returned from Bethel to prepare for his arrival. He will be coming here in three days with the whole entourage of prophets!" he yelled back.

This was good news! As I strolled back along the paths that led to our home, I felt like a bird that has just been released from its cage. Unfortunately, the light-hearted feeling didn't last long and those few days dragged painfully by. Finally, the third day dawned and I left the house in the early hours of the morning, fearful of missing him. I headed quickly for the road coming from Bethel and found a comfortable spot under a tree with a clear view and sat down to wait.

My eyes remained fixed on the furthest shimmering pin-point of highway before it disappeared between the foothills. Every now and then someone from the town passed by and greeted me, but I had little desire for idle talk; I was too pent up with a mixture of hope and doubt, and these fickle feelings played havoc with me as they soared and dipped. One moment that distant thruway carried the golden promise of the saving grace of God, and the next the tortuous shackles of the very pit of despair. The hours crept by, and it became difficult even to pray, for my thoughts were far too disjointed and distracted. So passed the longest day I think I have ever lived through.

Late in the afternoon, that narrow ribbon of highway completely disappeared behind a large gathering of people heading my way. Then I recognized Elisha; his formidable presence was even more intimidating than usual among such an elect group of attendants. Suddenly, scared stiff but resolute, I stood up and shook the dust off my skirts; the moment had come, and I had to make the best of it. My heart pounded wildly, and I'm sure I looked even wilder with worry. I certainly felt that way! The first words of greeting wobbled woefully, but they grew in strength as I cried out.

"Your servant my husband is dead, and you know that he revered the Lord. But now his creditor is coming to take my two boys as his slaves."

Then he asked, "How can I help you?"

Hearing these uplifting words was like receiving a long, cool drink after days of dry and dusty thirst, and I battled to overcome an intense and sudden desire to cry. He, seeing this, added quickly and gently, "Tell me, what do you have in your house?"

"Your servant has nothing there at all, except a little oil," I barely managed to utter, not daring to look at him in my despair.

"Go around and ask all your neighbors for empty jars. Don't ask for just a few. Then go and shut the door behind you and your sons. Pour oil into all the jars, and as each is filled, put it to one side," he ordered kindly.

Confused, I stared at him for a moment, but I wasn't prepared to question such a man, so I turned and fled to do as he asked. All I remember is that it felt as though I had wings instead of legs. Once home I waited impatiently for the boys to return, pacing the floor feverishly, and thinking how strange life can be. It is such a queer mix of joy and pain, the commonplace and the unexpected.

Uzi yanked the door open and, catching sight of me, said in an unusually deep tone as if he'd been practicing, "Hi, Mom. We're home. What's up?" I nearly laughed out loud but caught myself in time. It wouldn't do to hurt his feelings. Instead, I simply told them what Elisha had said to do.

Before thinking, he began to protest, "What's the point of that? We'd barely wet the bottom of each." The unguarded moment cost him, for his voice broke midway and ended on its old childish note.

Ben's face broke into a wide grin and he cried, "Can't you see? God is going to fill the jars!"

Uzi was about to counter this when he hesitated. "God's going to … perform a miracle," he said, testing the words to be sure. And then exhilaration took hold and he roared, "What are we waiting for?" The two of them rushed off to collect all the largest containers from our unsuspecting neighbors, creating quite a stir amongst these generous contributors.

When this was done, I obediently closed the door, shutting out the curious. And then, conscious of my every move, went to get what was left of our oil from the cupboard. The pot looked unbelievably tiny in comparison to the miscellaneous assortment of empty ceramic jars covering the floor. The boys had certainly done their job well! This was the moment of reckoning, and we stood together in a little knot of tense excitement, for we were not sure quite what to expect.

Two pairs of eyes stared fixedly at me, willing me on as, with just a hint of unsteadiness, I reached out towards the nearest empty vessel. The trembling increased and rapidly became uncontrollable, even as the oil slid slowly out over the small lip of the little pot. I was in real danger of spilling all the precious liquid. At that moment, Uzi's hand shot out and covered mine, whereupon the oil splashed a safe and sure golden path down and landed on the large empty ceramic base, and then spread out with long yellow, greedy fingers, twisting and swelling, until these joined again into one uniform whole that slowly crept higher and higher up the sides of the pot until it was filled to the brim.

It was so quiet in the room you could hear the sound the oil made as it hit the floor of each jar! There are no words to describe how we felt as we watched that tiny bit of oil fill each jar slowly, surely.

I waited impatiently for Uzi to bring me the next jar. When he didn't budge, I turned to him and said, "Bring me another one." The words, like the blows of a hammer, pounded the silence, striking harshly on our eardrums. My older son stared uncomprehendingly at me for a few seconds before gazing at all the jars filled with gleaming golden oil.

"There's not a jar left," he whispered.

As he spoke the oil stopped flowing and we were left gaping wide-mouthed at the richly glinting liquid gold. There was enough to pay a king's ransom! And then suddenly, spontaneously, we all burst out laughing. The boys started cavorting like overgrown puppies around the jars, singing "We're rich, we're rich!"

"Be careful," I cautioned as I sank down on the floor, content just to take in the miracle before me.

After a while the words the boys were chanting registered. *They're right*, I thought. *We are rich; really rich! There is more than enough oil, and what am I to do with the surplus oil once the debt is cleared? It really isn't mine to keep.* Then out of the blue a horrible desire to do nothing and say nothing, to just secretly hoard it all, consumed me. *After all*, argued my capricious mind, *Elisha said to collect as many jars as we could, and all we've done is be obedient; it isn't my fault there is a surplus. Surely God could have stopped the flow of oil anytime He'd wanted to.*

And then it hit me like a lightning bolt. Of course He could have, but He'd chosen not to. It really wasn't about the miracle—amazing as it was; it was all about Him, about His love for us. That was the moment when I truly realized I only needed God. Full of thankfulness, I sat silently contemplating His great love and repenting of the greed.

Before long I knew what I had to do. I settled the boys and quietly and deliberately told them my intentions. Then I left them guarding the oil while I rushed off to find Elisha.

Once out of their sight, the strange new temptation I'd experienced earlier returned. *Why,* argued my mind, *do I have to bother Elisha? He's probably busy with important business and won't want to be disturbed. If I sell all the oil, our future will be secure; the boys won't have to work so hard, and we'll be free from worry. Surely this must be God's intention by blessing us so liberally? Isn't this all a little unnecessary? Perhaps all I am doing by going to Elisha is proving to the boys how right I am.*

This last part hit home and I hesitated. Perhaps I am being a little self-righteous. I almost turned back at this point when I thought, *what about Elisha? Doesn't he have a right to know what has happened? How awful if he found out some other way?* This settled the issue for me and I hurried on, determined to let him decide what to do with the extra oil, for I didn't want to feel like a thief in the face of God's generosity.

"Man of God," I said when I found him. "What you told us to do we have done, and God has saved my sons from slavery. We have more than enough oil to pay back the debt. What should we do with all the rest?"

He smiled and said, "Go sell the oil and pay your debts. You and your sons can live on what is left."

With great joy and a profound sense of freedom, I left him to do just that! So this is my story of being tested and tried by God through devastating loss and amazing provision. I hope it has encouraged you.

Daughter of the Father

"As they pass through the Valley of Baka [weeping],
they make it a place of springs"
—Psalm 84:6a

"Hey! What're you laughin' at? Just wait 'til I catch you; then you'll have somethin' to laugh at!" Her brother rose clumsily and, correcting his balance with a quick half-step backwards, jabbed his ankle on a sharp, stumpy twig jutting out the side of the log he'd used for a seat. He let out a yell; the hurt foot involuntarily jerked forward and tipped the milk bucket. He lunged downwards, catching the swaying pail in time to stop the milk slopping over onto the dirt, but not in time to avoid being nicked on the wrist by a stray hoof as the cow indignantly shifted position.

Another peel of laughter hit the air.

"Blast!" He moved the bucket out of harm's way and rubbed the reddening spot quickly. Then he spun around and charged for her. Still laughing, she darted off across the spacious backyard as fast as her legs would carry her, startling the small herd of speckled and spotted goats ambling toward them and scattering them in all directions as they fled, bleating, for shelter. The ground tore away from under her feet as she made for the donkey grazing contentedly by himself over to the left of the plot. She dashed around the animal and turned warily to face her pursuer. They eyed one another, panting a little to catch their breaths, the bulky body of the old donkey a safe barrier between them. The donkey cast a suspicious sideways glance at both of them, and then snorted indignantly as if to say "Not again!" After a quick flick of his long ears to further express displeasure, he bent his disapproving, shaggy head and consoled himself with a thick tuft of dandelion.

"Catch me if you can. Come on, catch me if yon can," she taunted over and over, with an unmistakable glee.

Her brother threw her a look that spoke volumes and then darted to the right. She flew to the left. Every move he made, she parried. Although two years his junior, she was as watchful as a bird and as quick as lightning on her feet.

Their father stepped through the open door and leant back against the sturdy post. The expression in his eyes softened while he watched them. His daughter was so agile now she could keep up this game of tag all day if she wanted to, but he knew her favorite part was when she was caught and tickled. He often suspected, these days, that she allowed her brothers to catch her. He chuckled, as his son spun awkwardly this way and that. He was still playing catch-up with his own limbs, let alone hers. Finally, the giggling girl stalled and the boy managed to grab her. It was as the man suspected!

Although the peak of summer was over, the evening was still delightfully warm and the light, bright and clear, when they all gathered hungrily around the kitchen table to eat. The father blessed the meal and then sat back, taking in his kids as they tucked, with ravenous gusto, into the tasty food. Less than two years difference between each of them, their youthful faces were constantly changing and maturing. All four were growing up – and fast! His oldest son was a man now, at almost eighteen, he reckoned, scratching his head thoughtfully. Playful remarks bounced back and forth across the table like a volley of verbal balls as the youngsters joked together. He sighed contentedly. The year following his wife's death sure was a struggle, but this past year much less so – in fact, thanks to his kids' high-spirited fun, the long and golden summer days were almost magical. The fast-disappearing food began to satisfy stomachs and, out of habit, four pairs of eyes fixed expectantly on him. The girl smiled happily. This was her most favorite time of the day, when dad would tell them another miraculous story about God and their people.

The young girl hastened to prepare lunch. Her father and oldest brother had just, unexpectedly, arrived back from their trip to sell grain at the annual harvest market. This event was held yearly at a neighboring town. Although no explanation was given for their sudden return, she could tell from the tension in the air that something unusual had happened. She cut the bread into thick chunks, and then stared with frustration at the soup. It was taking its sweet time to cook!

The man was relieved that the unpleasant task of notifying his neighbors was over. It never felt good to be the bearer of bad news. He stared uneasily down at the dwindling pile of logs. The fall air was growing nippier and there were not too many weeks left before the cold weather really settled in. Now that all the grain was harvested and stored, he and the boys really needed to turn their attention to stock-piling wood. But this small worry was not what really perturbed him. The wood would have to wait. It was that interaction he'd had with his brother, when he'd grabbed hold of his arm and pulled him aside from bagging grain for satisfied buyers, that was the real cause of his disquiet. He shivered as he recalled the harsh urgency in Nathan's features that had made his face almost as unrecognizable as his voice.

"Bro, I'm so glad to see you. I've bad news! Yesterday, a couple of raiders were spotted, scouting out the territory in the hills just to the north of us. We're no idea how big the main pack is, but we can be sure, from some of the reports that have been trickling down over the summer from Gath-hepher and Endor, that there's a ton of them. But, there's no way of knowing where they'll go or what towns they'll attack. We are all vulnerable. It is best to be prepared for the worst."

The news was startling, but before he could collect his thoughts a group of elders, assembled on a small podium, shushed the crowd. He glanced expectantly at them, hoping for more information.

"There'll be no announcement," whispered his brother, anticipating the direction of his thoughts. "They're only up there to introduce the old prophet from Bethel who arrived in town a couple of days back. They respect the man and hope a good report will raise our spirits at this critical time."

"No announcement! Surely not, if this news is true, they'll have to make an announcement!"

Nathan vigorously shook his head, "The elders have decided that a one-on-one report is the best way of informing the men. This way the crowd won't panic. At noon, Josef, the town-crier, will make an official announcement to those still here. But, there's no need to wait for that.

There's nothing more to learn other than what I've already told you. You'll want to leave right away to speed up your preparations."

He looked apprehensively around and noticed a few men already hitching their donkeys to carts. Obviously they had no intention of staying for the pending speech.

"I think I'll hear out the old man first," he said slowly, still absorbing the disturbing info. Despite King Ahab's wickedness, God's evident blessing on Elijah, the prophet, and upon the godly Jehoshaphat, the Judean king, had brought the two kingdoms many years of peace, and the untroubled years had made him almost forget what it felt like to live in fear of a possible invasion. After Ahab's death, his grand-son Joram clung to the Asherah pole and many in Israel followed his example and worshipped pagan gods, despite the many miracles God performed through Elijah and Elisha. He'd often wondered whether this practice, in the face of so many demonstrations of God's power, would make Israel once again vulnerable to their enemies, and now it looked as though it had.

Nathan bent closer, almost spitting in his ear in his haste to speak, "Well then, have it your way, but you can't say I didn't warn you. So…. then, this is goodbye, Bro. I'll be leaving now, for we've much to do yet to get ready." He jerked away and then hesitated, fighting for control. He spun around and gripped his hand hard. "I'm scared bro; we're bitterly in need of a few extra days. If they attack to-night or tomorrow, we're done for!"

"Nathan, remember our God and remember his miracles; he's the one who's really in control – not the raiders, not the Asherah or even the Baals! Our lives are in Yahweh's hands. He'll rescue you from them, but even if he doesn't, trust in him. He'll be with you always; He'll never leave you, or your wife, or the little ones." His voice was calm and strong, and, in that moment, he knew he believed this, unreservedly.

"Bro, you're the best brother a feller can have. That's a good reminder. Pray for us, even as we will for you. God keep you all safe!" Nathan cried, hugging him fiercely.

He'd stayed out of respect for the bent, elderly man, but even the astonishing account the prophet gave of Elisha's latest miracle, where a hundred men were fed from only twenty small loaves of barley bread, faded before the more alarming news.

The unguarded years had rendered them nearly defenseless and, if the report of raiders was true and there was no reason to doubt it wasn't, an attack on their town could be imminent. There was no way of knowing what might happen to his community now that they'd slackened up so much. Or, God willing, they might continue to be spared. *But regardless of which, our first and most pressing need, is to prepare weapons,* he mused. *We'll have to haul out the swords and spear heads from the cellar and then convert our hoes into spears and sharpen the rusty swords. Fortunately, with five ready pairs of hands, this shouldn't take more than a day to complete.* He surveyed the adjacent homes behind their screen of pine trees, and glimpsed a few neighbors scurrying to and fro, probably with the same tasks in mind. He knew the news he'd passed on would spread like wild-fire. Soon a watch would be stationed on the walls and on the mount behind the town. He felt another shiver of foreboding and quickly collected an armful of wood. His daughter stuck her head out the door and hollered that lunch was ready.

There's no sense in disturbing the family with this news until after we've eaten, he decided as he trundled back to the welcome warmth of the house. *Let's first enjoy the meal and the latest miracle. Whatever horrors the future holds for us, a strong faith in God is the surest way to survive the ordeal.* Opening the door to the small, crowded room he was greeted by jovial banter along with the smell of fresh roasted bread. The lanky bodies of his sons seemed to fill every corner as he gazed around, and he wondered for the umpteenth time how his young daughter managed, in such a tight space, to create the amazing concoctions that daily fed their impatient hunger.

True to his earlier decision, it was only after they'd cleared away the dishes that he called attention to the urgent need to prepare weapons. Instantly this news, like water to a fire, dampened the festive mood. Various tasks were assigned to each member of the family, and soon they were laboring away at these. Some hours later, the small pile of ready weaponry still looked pitiably thin, for it only boasted one completed spear, a sharpened sword and a couple of daggers. *There is so much more to do yet!* Thought the man edgily as he eyed the finished product. *Darkness has crept upon us too quickly; it will be a miracle if we finish preparing all the weapons to-night.* He stepped quickly outside on the pretext of collecting more wood for the fire, but really it was to hide the agitation he felt from the others. *O Lord, we are in desperate need of your help.* He took a deep breath and surveyed the silvery-gray landscape under its star-studded, moonlit canopy. The fires twinkling from the windows of the adjoining homes felt immensely reassuring. Thin plumes of smoke pointed long, encouraging fingers towards the God of the heavens. Everything appeared remarkably still and tranquil, even the animals were quiet and at rest. Is this the calm before the storm, he wondered apprehensively, feeling again that disquieting shiver.

In the wee hours of morning, when the stack of weapons had tripled impressively, and tired-out youth slept soundly, the father sat on alone, listening to the soft, cascading breaths and the occasional snap of a dying ember. He could not shake off the depressing feeling that tomorrow would bring unwelcome change. He fell to his knees, a desperate urgency propelling him to pray that, whatever befell them, he and his children would stand firm in faith and face the enemy with courage. It was not until the darkness outside began to lighten that he stood stiffly to his feet. He felt utterly spent but strangely at peace; come what may, he could rest in God's providence. He reached over and removed the flint-box from the shelf above the fireplace. He lifted back the lid on its hinges and took out the two rough flint-stone fire-starters and placed them back on the shelf. His restless fingers searched the base of the narrow box. They found a small lever, shifted this across to one side and then lifted up a false bottom to reveal a shallow niche. He stood motionless; the lines scoring his face deepened as he gazed down at the snug contents. Sweet memories, born from a depth of love he could not have believed possible, flooded back. For a brief moment, the loss of the past and the heavy stress of the present nearly overwhelmed him and he almost snapped the lid shut. But something stayed his hand. He drew a deep breath and gently pulled out a gem-studded necklace, the last, remaining reminder of his dead wife. He walked quickly over to a chest standing beside his cot and rummaged through the thin layers of clothing. In no time at all he found the tunic he was looking for. He felt for a small opening in the hem and then, with a quick prayer, slid the trinket between the double layers of material. He shook the fabric so that the necklace slid over to the far side where no-one would notice it and then deftly slipped the garment over his head. He touched the corner housing the necklace and sighed deeply, content that he would not be separated from this most precious memory of his dear wife.

This satisfaction, however, was short-lived. An image of his youngest child's sweet and expectant smile instantly brought back the earlier furrows. What would happen to her? What if he was killed and this valuable necklace was buried with him and, God-forbid, she was captured; or worse yet, stranded with no means of support? He undressed slowly; perhaps his beloved wife's trinket might, somehow, prove to be of more use to her, than to him. When she awoke, he would ask her to hang onto the tunic for safe-keeping. It was all he could think of doing. Suddenly he felt very old and weary.

The sharp clash of steel upon steel pierced through the roar of crashing and burning timber, deafening ears and setting teeth on edge. The leaping flames forced the ill-equipped women and children out of their hiding-holes and into the thick of battle. They scurried about, choking and squealing like a pack of crazed rats. Within minutes, a bulky, shadowy form emerged from under the mantle of churning charcoal smoke and tossed-up embers, deliberately but guardedly detaching itself from the ferocious slaughter. Soon, only thin wisps of smoke clung like ghostly hands around his legs as he slunk past half-charred bodies scattered amongst smoldering beams, filling the air with the all too familiar pungent stench of scorched flesh. His progress was hampered only by the large, motionless bundle slung over his powerful shoulders. Sly eyes glinted above the damp cloth covering his nose and mouth as he glanced swiftly about the blackened fringes of the burning town. So far this had been a successful raid, and he wasn't going to allow any surprise attack to change that.

It was agreed that the spoils from all the raids be pooled and then, when the fighting was done, distributed according to merit amongst the surviving officers and warriors. His mind drifted back to the earlier sedition that augmented this decision. After days of trudging over what felt like innumerable mountains yet white with snow, it took all their combined strength to hold back the chariots, still harnessed to the horses, as they descended the steep face of the canyon to the swollen creek below. Then the heavy chariots had to be lifted up and carried over the turbulent spring waters. They lost quite a few men and a couple of good horses to the swiftly flowing waters. His cousin was one of them, and his mouth tightened as he remembered the man.

Once across, the ascent up the ravine was equally difficult. The men were deathly weary by the time they made it to the top. Then all hell broke loose. The attack was swift and vicious, surprising them—decimating their troops, reducing them by a third of their original number, before they eventually gained the upper hand. Then the leader of the Ammonites urged a quick retreat and the band of horsemen turned about and fled. The relieved Arameans barely gave chase before flopping down exhausted among the rocks close to the slain, oblivious to the blood and filth that still testified of the earlier horror—too weary even to lift a muscle to loot the unfortunate dead.

All that evening as they set up camp in the dark the men were subdued from the enormity of the loss. By the morning, however, the grumbling began in earnest. Rosjon's voice was the loudest.

"We did not come all this way to become meat for those thugs of herdsmen to carve at their will. We're suppose to pillage them—not the vandals us! We can't rely on the trackers to warn us in time. Our commander should have known better. He should have realized that we were heading into a trap. Now many of our mates lie dead and he's to blame. They were good warriors; if it weren't for their bravery, we might all be lying in the dust with our throats cut, feeding the vultures. I say we ditch this lot and head on home before more of us die."

The disgruntled raiders swarmed about him like wasps, relieved to find one who would give voice to their unarticulated feelings.

"Anyway, we get precious little reward for all this effort!" he cried bitterly. "Does the king care what happens to us? Do we mean anything to him beyond the fact that we furnish his army with a steady supply of horses, his wives with a steady supply of slaves, and his chests with the best pickings of the treasures? I ask you all—how much are our lives worth to the king besides making him rich? I'll tell you—not a dog's tail! The king does not give a damn what happens to us! It's not fair that plunder so hard won is claimed by the king and that we have to wait for him to dish us out a morsel. We sweat—we bleed for it—it should all be ours!"

A roar of approval met these words, and two men lifted him high onto their shoulders. Fueled by this support, he shouted on.

"It's our blood we spill, not his. We need to stand together. That way we can become strong and put an end to this abuse. I vote we grab the horses, the rest of the supplies and all the loot, and push off home before more of us die. We've taken the risks and sacrificed our lives for this. It's ours by right."

The mood became ugly as the passions of the listening horde were aroused. They raised their fists in the air and began to chant Rosjon's name. Always an unruly lot, their loyalty was easily lost and won. All it required was for one man in the midst of a grievance to rise up and pour salt on the wound for the pack to desert the old dog and follow after the new. However, once gaining their fickle allegiance, it took a firm hand to hold them in check. Then a powerful voice bellowed across the clamour.

"These are seditious words—words which, if reported to the king, will cost you your necks."

The shouting halted as the uncertain mob turned to face a tall and commanding figure of a man standing atop a chariot, supported by a group of officers with drawn swords.

"But only if the report gets through to him. We can make sure that never happens," snarled a gruff voice. This threat sparked a similar run of threats. Rosjon, towering above the men and still caught up in a passion of furious eloquence, pulled out his dagger and pointed it menacingly.

"You hear what the men say. Better to live than to die. If you want to live, drop your swords and fall in with us. We're not going to be dictated to by an absent king, who won't even shed his blood and sweat with us. We're going to band together as brothers and become a formidable force—a force that will look after the interests of the common man and not those of kings. Look to your weapons, men!"

With wild cries and whistles, the seething protesters brandished daggers—and the occasional sword—and closed ranks. The commander laughed derisively and lifted his hand, silencing the hostile horde.

"Have your way and the officers and I will make sure there are precious few of you left to enjoy the spoils. Behind us, envoys are mounted, ready to ride at my word," he growled. "All the horses are hitched together and these couriers will make sure they reach the king safely. Those of you who survive this skirmish will be left stranded, without the quick means of escape you hope for. You will live as hunted men, always on the run, afraid for your lives."

For a brief moment his words cowed the rabble and they swore uneasily under their breaths. Then fresh assertions and accusations erupted, feeding their angry frustration until this, once again, threatened to burst the bounds of reason.

"But wait! Listen to me! I have a better idea than treason and another blood bath," yelled the commander, his strong voice like a trumpet blast above the volatile din. "One that I guarantee will avoid more bloodshed and benefit you all, not just the king! My plan will give you and your families a hope and a future. None of you will have to slink about like a fugitive, terrified of shadows."

"Don't listen to him," yelled Rosjon, suddenly frightened for his life as he observed the mob's hesitation. "These are nothing but lies! We will all be charged with treason, and the officers will hand us over to the king on our return. We will all die!"

This had the desired effect, and the dissenters exploded once again into foul protest.

"Not one of you will be handed over to the king; you have my word," roared the commander above the wild hostility. His voice dropped persuasively to a lower key. "I challenge those of you who are so quick to grumble to live up to your words. You shall prove your boldness through acts of valour."

The commander's words struck the right chord and the uproar stilled as the men began to listen.

"I am of the same opinion as yourselves, that those of you who prove the most valiant in the raids should be rewarded the most," he declared. That this was not strictly their gripe did not deter the man at all. He had their eager attention, and now he could play his hand. "So this is the plan. I propose that the loot be pooled, with all the horses and one tenth of the spoil going to the king."

Some of the interested but still disgruntled rabble instantly disputed this, and again he quieted them with his hand. Then he leapt down and strode into the centre of the mob, splitting it in half as the men backed away. This brave action dampened the last of the wild fire in their eyes, even those holding up Rosjon, and they silently lowered him to the ground.

"The rest of the spoils will be divided among us all at the end of the raiding," he continued, the crowd hanging onto every word like a pack of tame wolves eating from the hand of their master. "We will hold an award ceremony and celebrate the valour of those remaining according to merit. No partiality will be shown; each will get his fair share, according to his deeds, and the bravest among you will be awarded the rank of an officer. Those of you who are in favour, lift your hands in a show of support."

The unanimous response to the proposal suited the raider. He had no desire to be a deserter. His plans were bigger than that. The commander, he figured, was a man who could, like himself, seize an opportune moment. And what an opportune moment this was, for it left the door wide open for advancement. Now the season when men go to war was drawing to a close, and as this was the last of the planned raids, he was making sure—very sure—that he was one of the men who received his reward that evening.

A soft groan filtered through the thick folds of fabric draped over his back and the sound caused him to pick up the pace. Sweat poured down his forehead in rivulets, drowning his eyes. He blinked rapidly; he would have to rest soon, but only when it was safe. A couple of dogs not far from him licked at a pool of blood, and then snarled as he darted past. He cursed them under his breath as he wound a path through hacked and smashed rubble to reach the flimsy protection of a recently torched barn.

In a dark corner of the barely standing and still smoldering skeleton, he carefully lay his wriggling but well bound bundle on the ground and hurriedly untied the ropes. *This was good plunder—tunics and shawls of the best quality*, he thought, lifting each individual piece up to the dim light before carefully laying it down. *And the girl … especially the girl.* He smacked his lips with satisfaction as he pulled aside the last of the beautifully woven garments to reveal the attractive youngster. She flinched in pain, blinking up at him. Grabbing the silk scarf from about his neck, he deftly stuffed it into her opening mouth, muffling her screams before they had a chance to air. *Yes, and very marketable, too. She's young … still as flat as a boy, but not quite.* He leaned over and inspected her rigid body before staring hard into her pinched and traumatized eyes. A cruel smile twisted his grim lips.

She clutched for the discarded clothing by her side and drew it back over herself protectively. His small eyes lit lustfully, the fear emanating from her fuelling some perverse pleasure. The fact that this plunder wasn't technically his didn't mean he couldn't have some fun first, he decided, savouring the mastery of the moment as he watched her pitiful efforts to hide from his leer. He'd have his way with her now, before anyone else. He pulled the garment clear of her tight-fisted grasp, fingering the soft richness of the material. Something metallic slid through his fingers and bunched into a corner of the piece of clothing. Grabbing the material, he lifted it up to investigate further and then carefully extracted a golden necklace from its hiding place deep within the lining of the hem. He held it up, clear of the shadows. The piece was intricately cast and embedded with multi-colored precious stones. Each perfectly cut jewel caught alight like fire as it twirled in a silent dance under the streaming beams of diffused light. His eyes gleamed covetously and he whistled under his breath, absorbing the trinket's magical beauty. Here was a rare prize indeed!

This exquisite find would also have to go into the general pot—an idea that became less and less attractive the longer he eyed the shimmering jewels. His glance shifted about for a suitable hiding place. Perhaps he could bury it somewhere and come back for it later. Then his brow crinkled. What if some sneak followed him when he came to retrieve it? If his comrades discovered the theft, they would hang him for unlawful possession. He stroked his beard rhythmically, keeping an eye on the girl, as he deliberated. What if he returned the trinket to its hiding place? No one would know it was there. Then, when it was his turn to be acknowledged during the ceremony for valiant exploits, he could legitimately select the tunic as part of his reward. Then later—much later—he would "find" the treasure, and none would be the wiser. The more obviously valuable goods would be selected first, so there might be a chance that by the time his name was announced, it would still be available. He eyed the garment doubtfully. The fabric was of a fine quality and the garment well made. What if someone else grabbed it first? Could he risk that?

Perhaps he could swing a deal. His eyes narrowed to thin speculative slits as they moved from one prize to the other. What if he presented the girl to the commander, before she became part of the general pool of slaves? All he sought in return was to be allowed to choose his reward earlier in the ceremony, along with the best warriors. It wasn't as if he didn't deserve the honour. This plunder was surely worthy of a king and more than enough evidence of his skill. And ... a deal like this might mark the beginning of a long understanding that was mutually favourable. Such an advantageous connection might even lead to a promotion in the near future. Imagine being ... an officer! The staggering idea momentarily startled him, cooling his rising passion and fuelling instead the polluted coals of dark ambition. He rocked back on his heels to consider the implications of this action. Yes, but then he'd have to leave her alone, he thought sourly. He raked his eyes once more over the petrified girl.

She certainly was worthy of gracing a commander's household ... or better yet, his own. He studied the trinket dubiously. The gems sparkled tauntingly, mockingly, fanning the craving for acquisitiveness into full-blown, insatiable greed. The girl, he at last decided, was dispensable; there would be many more like her. But not this trinket—there was only one of its kind. He had to have this treasure at any cost! He returned the necklace to its hiding place. A smirk tugged the corners of his mouth down as he turned the tunic inside out, rendering it less attractive to the eye. He was taking a risk, but the odds of the scheme succeeding were high. The commander was, after all, only a man like himself, and each man had his price. Once a bargain was struck, this priceless gem would unquestioningly be his.

But what if the gamble failed and he lost not just the girl, but everything? He scratched his sweat begrimed brow indecisively. Yes, that might prove irksome, but he was fairly resourceful. If no other solution could be found, he was not above using more persuasive methods. He'd watch and wait until an opportunity presented itself and then, if needs be, forcefully take what was his by right. Either way, he couldn't lose!

The young girl stood apprehensively beside the stranger. She wriggled her dry tongue around until it felt more normal and then carefully wet her cracked lips, conscious of a dull pain somewhere at the base of her skull. Instinctively she raised her bound hands to investigate and with difficulty found the spot and rubbed it gently. The smoke laden wind blew a few stray strands of auburn hair across her forehead where they stuck to suspiciously wet lashes. The tightly bound hands were quickly employed to brush these away. Then she spat into the long grass, in an attempt to get rid of the unpleasant taste the grubby scarf had left behind in her mouth. The man moved closer and a tremor of terror dilated her pupils, darkening the cherry-brown irises to black. She shuddered as she stole a quick glance at him. *I'm so scared! Where are you, Dad?*

The raider secured her with rope to himself and then yanked hard on his end, causing her to almost fall flat on her face as he took off. Without any further mishap they reached the base of the mountain towering over the torched town, where he started to climb swiftly up a steep embankment. It required all of her strength and youthful agility to match his practiced adult stride. The air was still thick with smoke, and it took a bit of strenuous climbing before they were high enough to breathe easily.

She gulped the fresh air gratefully; it was hard going to keep pace with the man. From far below the shrill clang of sparring swords followed by the occasional blood-curdling scream sent shivers down her spine. Finally, he jerked her to a halt on a shelf of soft scrub behind a natural wall of rock. From this advantageous position, they watched the final act of the brutal combat in the recently harvested fields below the stone walls of the smoldering town.

"I reckon Dad and the boys are in the thick of it," she whispered with a sudden surge of pride as the skirmishing raged relentlessly on.

Clouds of choking dust and drifting smoke shrouded the fighting figures in dusty-grey fog, making it difficult for her straining eyes to pick out any familiar form. A horn blew faintly in the distance, and pairs of archers standing tall upon iron chariots appeared on the rise and stormed down the slope, leaving behind rivulets of sand as they sped towards the hazy battlefield.

"Dad, oh Dad," she cried helplessly. Her youthful pride shifted into dark despair as more and more bodies buckled and fell to the bloodied earth. Even as the dreadful necropolis of the slain mushroomed about the fields, her mind screamed against the injustice.

The taut rope jerked hard, rasping against the tender torso, but elicited no reaction. Her captor half-turned and scowled, even as a whip sang nimbly through the air sending its palpable message swiftly up to her numbed brain. The pain of the immediate present stilled the awful, impotent protest, and she turned automatically, dully, to follow his quick descent. She stared disbelievingly down at the wrecked remains of the blackened buildings in the smoke-filled valley, trying to absorb this new and unfamiliar landscape. Everything felt bizarre, out of this world; reality distorted into the grim and grotesque—a living nightmare!

Yes ... that's it! Perhaps it's all just a horrible dream. She shot another frightened look at the unflinching profile above hers. The harsh contour with the defining hatchet nose and tight-lipped mouth, just visible above a thick and scraggly beard, split the delusion into shreds. No, it was no illusion; he was very real!

Hatchet! Her mind played with the word. Yes, that's a good name for the brute! The next moment her feet tripped and the ready whip sliced the air again.

"Ouch, that hurt!" she muttered fiercely, fighting back the quick sting of tears.

She braced thin shoulders and focused on the path before them. Muddled thoughts of somehow escaping this wild fiend rolled untidily over and over in her mind like tangled tumble-weed. A root snared her foot and she stumbled blindly. The rope instantly tightened. She felt again the burn of rough twine wearing her skin raw, even as the whip whistled. It missed its target fractionally and she quickly readjusted her steps.

Wafts of smoke carrying random fiery sparks drifted over from a burning farmhouse. Her eyes smarted and she turned her face to escape the acrid fumes. The bloodied bodies of a man lying alongside a woman whose gouged stomach exposed a half-formed baby made the world swim suddenly, sickeningly, and she vomited into the long grass as she staggered on. The surreal numbing sensation of a dream mercifully came back.

Soon they were joined by other men carrying plunder. Among them were other unlucky captives. One of the men brushed against a shadowy bush and he swore loudly as the shadow morphed into a youth who tore away through the scrub. The man charged after him, returning shortly with the boy bound even as she was. They exchanged glances and something about this tense but expressive face reminded her of her brother's.

The summer sun had bowed low in the mournful violet-red sky when they almost caught up with three men who'd steadily plodded ahead of them for the last hour, pulling a heavily laden cart. Suddenly the one pushing at the rear paused and threw a knife up into an overhanging branch. Then the air was rent by a blood-curdling cry. She shuddered with fright, even as a wounded man sprang down and fell heavily upon the two in front, stabbing a knife deeply into each as they collapsed under his weight. The remaining marauder with a fluid, lightning-quick pounce, descended upon the attacker and plunged his sword through him and then, as quickly, yanked out the blood-stained weapon and thrust it back into the sheath hanging loosely at his side. He spun round, shouting something undecipherable. Hatchet immediately yelled back, and raucous laughter rippled among the men. She gasped, stunned by this cold-blooded response to such ruthless slaughtering. Were they men or just animals?

Ignoring the pitiful cries of the only survivor, others from their group leapt forward and began to strip the mutilated bodies of weapons and valuables. The rest moved on, disregarding the activity of those left behind and, glancing backwards, she saw the looters dump the dead and dying like carrion by the side of the road before hauling the cart away. Presently they came upon the main pack of Aram hunters busily setting up camp under a grove of olive trees. Archers astride a couple of iron chariots drove up with a flourish, causing a pair of horses tethered nearby to rise up on their hind legs and whinny nervously before settling peacefully to pull at clumps of sweet grass. She dejectedly surveyed the alien commotion, aware that a new and terrifyingly unfamiliar page had turned in the story of her young life.

Hatchet swaggered up to the commander's pavilion and halted before the guard manning the entrance. His general approach was to bully or coerce, depending on the type of man he confronted. He sized up the one in front of him now with sharp, gimlet eyes and decided, incorrectly, to intimidate. Taking advantage of his few extra inches, he stared unpleasantly down his hooked nose at the official. Next, he unleashed the full power of his harsh voice and curtly demanded an audience with their leader. Then, without waiting for an answer, he dumped the large bundle of clothing expectantly down on the ground beside her cowering body.

The aide on duty eyed this action belligerently; he was in no mood to be accommodating. Also, he intensely disliked brow-beaters, and this one looked like he might top the list, he concluded, fighting back a strong desire to punch the ugly and sweaty visage. Schooling his features instead into the unreadable poker face that had been his salvation many times in similar situations, he began to issue a regal dismissal when the curtain covering the entrance was pulled aside. A powerful figure of a man emerged and the two men instantly bowed low. Their leader stared inscrutably for a moment at the two men before ignoring Hatchet and turning to the guard.

"Anything wrong?" he snapped sternly, his face wearing a look that demanded compliance.

"Nothing, Sir. Nothing that I can't deal with," promptly replied the man.

"Good," he said more mildly. He swung to go, even as Hatchet, realizing that he was about to lose this opportune moment, blurted out, "One moment, please, Commander!"

The man faced Hatchet impatiently. The girl peeked shyly at the commander's finely chiseled countenance. Here was a different calibre of man to her cruel enslaver. Instantly she wished it had been him, and not Hatchet, who'd captured her.

"Behold this prize plunder from today's raid, your Lordship!" The desire to boast was hard to suppress in the face of one so superior, and Hatchet, with a wide, sweeping gesture, theatrically indicated the pile of clothing and young girl. "If your Lordship were to cast his eye over the spoil, then I'm sure your Lordship would agree with me that this is indeed choice pickings, especially the girl!" Then, with a quick flick of his wrist, he jerked her to stand in front of their leader.

The commander's eyes swept from man to plunder, and a hint of contempt in the appraisal was banished so swiftly that the youngster could never be sure that it had ever been there. Then he waved imperiously towards the guard.

"My servant is well qualified to handle all your concerns."

Hatchet, blatantly disregarding the polite dismissal, bowed ingratiatingly before tilting the girl's face upwards. "Your Lordship, the only concern I have is to present to you this comely young slave. She is strong, healthy, and still as innocent as a child; she will make an excellent servant." Here he paused to take a deep breath before continuing. "Your Lordship only deserves the best. If this young slave pleases your Lordship, then your humble servant would be delighted if your Lordship will accept her as a gift for his household."

Their leader was instantly watchful, his eyes wary and calculating, reminding her forcefully of a lion before it pounces.

This is not a man to trifle with, she thought, experiencing a sudden qualm.

The guard watched this interaction with savage satisfaction. *I may yet have the satisfaction of planting my fist on that arrogant jaw,* he decided quietly.

Hatchet, impervious to these warning signs, preened his chest like a peacock before bumbling on. "If your Lordship is pleased with the gift, then perhaps, in return, your Lordship might keep me in mind when he considers who might be worthy of being honoured early on in the ceremony tonight."

With set jaw and ominously flashing eyes, the commander faced Hatchet squarely. "The scoundrel," he blazed within. "How dare he resort to flattery and bribery! Such an honour belongs only to those worthy of it. This rogue is decidedly unworthy, and *just* how unworthy he is will soon become plain to him!"

Hatchet's gaze wavered under this fierce look and shifted instead to rest uneasily on the guard's beaming face. The commander calmed himself with an effort. He was about to issue an order when he caught and held two large, pleading, and artlessly naive eyes, and hesitated.

Hatchet, observing the slight hesitation, wiped the sudden spurt of fresh sweat off his brow. He'd have to be more careful in the future. This man was no fool!

"But only if your Lordship should determine this success warrants such a prestigious acknowledgement," he finished lamely, sliding a sidelong glance at the girl.

He'd certainly not underestimated her charm. Since it was unlikely that the commander would look favourably on his offer, there was yet time to enjoy that childlike appeal. It would compensate, in part, for some of the humiliation he now felt. Fear flickered over her face as she shrank back from the meaning in his malicious eyes. The commander caught the tail-end of the unveiled leer and a swift revulsion filled his war-hardened heart. His cold eyes narrowed as he considered the rascal in front of him.

The youngster backed nervously up against the rough plaster and felt a sliver of mortar jab through the thin fabric of her new dress. Her pale, appealing face wore a new worldly- wise sharpness. She felt small and alone and still very afraid—afraid enough to feel her knees shaking under the plain cotton shift. Her big eyes were moist as they glanced around at the sea of alien faces, missing again the embracing warmth of the familiar.

Four weeks had passed since her capture and still the language was little more than babble. She scowled down at her bare toes scrunching the thick woolen strands of the Persian carpet. Every muscle felt strained and every nerve on edge. She pressed her hands hard against the wall to somehow avert the threatening avalanche of tears. It was a valiant effort, but her young face soon crumpled under an overwhelming rush of feelings as wave after wave of homesickness hit.

"God, oh God, help me," she sobbed silently.

Suddenly an image of Dad, fearless warm-hearted Dad, floated into her tortured mind. She was his girl and no matter what, whether he was alive or dead, she would not fail him. Serenity came from somewhere deep within, settling the raw emotions and filling her with renewed courage. She gazed shyly around the room, absorbing its beautiful and spacious proportions and the colorful inlaid tiles and plush drapes.

"I'm lucky I'm here and not with Hatchet." She shuddered at the name. This thought traced its way back home as so many did these days, and she furtively wiped away fresh tears.

"This will be a long and lonely day," she muttered under her breath and swallowed another sob.

Some emphasis in the loud guttural sounds brought her attention back to the head servant. He was pointing to some women clustered nearby as he rasped out orders. They turned as a whole to look at her. The sudden attention was as alarming as the meaning obscure. Then the oldest of the women smiled and held out her hand, beckoning her.

She stepped shyly forward.

After that first day, the morning assemblies within this hectic household became commonplace. Little of the meeting's full agenda applied, for her duties were simple and consisted mainly of helping the maids serve the great lady of the house. The work was pleasant enough, as was the easy banter. They both helped to lighten the dark hopelessness of those early weeks. Moreover, she liked being around the beautiful woman. Her voice was sweetly harmonious like chimes tinkling in the wind, and she had one of those warm and inclusive personalities which quickly captivate.

One unusually warm autumn afternoon, she sat with her feet idling in a pool of water, listening to the chit-chat on the far side of the courtyard. All the women, barring her, were enjoying the rare break in the day's duties. Most of the talk was now easily understandable, and she stifled a yawn, wishing she could be busy at some task to distract her mind from thinking about home. A scraping noise attracted her attention. She cocked her head on one side, her ears straining like that of a beloved pet dog for the sound of iron wheels grating against stone, signifying the return of the mistress's chariot.

A burst of laughter made her look up. Two of the younger girls were amusing themselves with some horse-play. This and every other interaction somehow reminded her of another time, another place. How it hurt to think of everyone back home, especially Dad. Back home? A cramp locked in her chest. There was no "home;" home had been reduced to cold, dead ashes blowing in the wind. The clear outlines of the patio blurred, and she bent her head quickly to avoid detection as large tears spilt over and onto the marble slabs skirting the water's edge. That day, like most of those early days, dragged on uneventfully until at last she was able to lay down on her narrow bed in the women's dorm and shut out the continual unfamiliarity and constant loneliness. Her eyes were wet with unshed tears as she drifted off to sleep.

She was running—running from something indescribably dark and ugly. Whichever way she turned, nameless horrors sprang up, until all her bones felt like liquid. Safety was somewhere ahead, but she couldn't move. The murderous darkness was gaining ground. It was coming closer … closer. The hair on her arms stood on end as it reached out to grab her in foul, reeking folds, pinning down her arms. Now she was struggling … and the dark cavernous mouth opened wide to suck her in …

Wild-eyed and hearing only the panicked thud of her heartbeat she fought against the suffocating tightness. Even as she pulled free and sat up, the monster became nothing other than the thick blanket coiled around her. She pushed it aside as though it were contaminated and then shivered, more from fear than the bite in the air. Quickly she curled up into a taut ball and stared fixedly at the dark, spidery shadows all around. Even the shallow breathing and occasional faint snores coming from the other women sleeping across the long and narrow room offered little comfort.

Gradually the crippling fear settled and she sensed instead the soothing peace that lately came after each terrifyingly repetitive dream. Strangely comforted, she listened to the gentle snores and watched the web-like patterns normalize into recognizable shapes. Eventually she became aware that she was cold. She touched the blanket tentatively. It felt fuzzy, normal, just like blankets should. She stretched out and pulled it back over her chilled body.

Dad, I miss you so much that it hurts. She lay still, remembering that last hug on that never to be forgotten day. Then other disturbing memories, full of stark horror, pushed aside this happy one, and she groaned in anguish.

"I hate all these people for what they've done to us!" she sobbed quietly. "I hate them!"

Hate hurts a person as much as leprosy. It rots them on the inside like leprosy rots them on the outside. The thought vibrated with the richness of her father's deep baritone and broke through the angry storm like a sunbeam on a dark and dismal day. She savoured the sound, considering the words. What does that mean? How does hate do that? And, as if in answer, another surprising idea, still clothed in that wonderful voice, lit her mind. *Forgiveness is like a cool drink of spring water refreshing the soul, but hatred is like drinking salt water. It only makes the thirst more desperate. It cannot satisfy.*

A struggle followed this perceptive revelation, and fresh tears freely flowed.

"It's not so easy, Dad, not to hate! Aren't I justified in hating them? Haven't they murdered you and enslaved me?" she whimpered into the blanket.

Nothing. No answering inspiration or thought came. The only apparent noise the soft, slumbering snoring that still drifted across the room, and she bawled into the blanket. Dad wasn't really with her. It was just her imagination conjuring up his voice and playing tricks on her. Strong feelings, overwhelming feelings, rose up like an unstoppable wave threatening to wipe out all desire to please his fast-fading memory.

"I can't forgive; I can't! It's too painful, and I'm too angry! I need someone to blame, to hate! I would destroy them if I could; just as they have destroyed us!"

If you destroy them, you become like them, doing the same hateful things they do, argued her conscience, summing up her former thoughts. But a woefully persistent and bitter feeling that she was nothing more than a victim, powerless and at the mercy of others, kept her in the womb of the angry wave, obscuring the truth.

"God's word says an eye for an eye!"

Her soft whisper resonated loudly in her ears, and the swell of the wave crested and broke, drowning all remaining argument. Triumphant now, she waited like a hawk ready to pounce on any contrary argument. But none came. Only the overpowering tides of revenge raged on within as the wintry-pale rays of dawn slowly lit the morning through the rough, rectangular frame of the window.

A flutter of wings made her glance up, and her bitter young features softened with a tiny smile. The slight movement caught the attention of a bright, black bead above a pale, yellow beak, and the little visitor adjusted its small, grey head to watch her unblinkingly for a few seconds from one wise, round eye before taking flight into the smudgy shades of pre-morning blue. Strangely, the room felt emptier after the exit of the dove. And then slowly, surprisingly, she became aware of another loss; the wonderful peace had gone. There was only an aching, awful lonesomeness.

Crushed, she stared unseeingly at the feeble promise of a bleak day whose light was gradually obliterating the shadows in the corners but not those crowding her miserable soul. She was truly alone—alone as never before. Not even when she was captured or had looked down at that awful battleground had she ever felt so utterly alone. She swallowed another sob. Why was life so hard? This unbearable loneliness was too much, too hopeless. Everything was utterly meaningless, and she didn't feel like living anymore!

"Dad, you are right," she said in a small voice. "Hating leaves nothing, and nothing is very, very lonely!"

These all consuming emotions were foreign to her normal happy disposition, and the effect was entirely negative; there were no redeeming qualities. *It isn't worth it*, she thought after a while. *How I must be disappointing Dad … and God, and somehow that's the worst of all.* The more she thought on this, the sadder she felt.

The weight of sorrow became unbearable. She turned face-down on the bed and wept bitterly into the blanket. All at once the room filled with a presence she could only sense. She lifted her head, the sobs instantly forgotten. The presence felt more present, more formidable, than any previous sensation of peace. God was, in some inexplicable way, in the room!

She felt acutely aware of her insignificance beside His greatness. Instinctively she knew He was waiting for a response from her. Everything inside her reached out to Him, and as she did the crippling anguish lifted and serenity past understanding soothed her troubled mind.

Over the following months, as an aging winter gave way to a youthful spring, the pain of loss lessoned, while her child-like faith in God strengthened. Not surprisingly, she found favour both with the mistress and with the other servants—except for one woman who had taken an inexplicable dislike to her.

I love this work, she thought, humming a catchy tune while surveying the beautiful room with the unabashed pleasure of youth. Everything was clean and in place.

"What's the tune you're humming?" asked a melodious voice. She spun around guiltily.

"Oh, it's nothing, just a tune I learnt back … home," she stammered. "I'm sorry if I was disturbing you, Mistress."

"Don't apologize; you weren't bothering me," reassured the lady quickly, conscious of the slight catch in the words. "It sounds so merry. Are there words to accompany the tune?"

"Yes," she said quickly recovering. "But they're in Hebrew."

"You can sing the song to me as you comb my hair and then tell me what it means," ordered the lady kindly.

She was quick to obey. This was one of her most favourite tasks, and only spoilt by the anxiety she noticed shadowing the woman's brow.

This shadow deepened over the following days and she sang other little ditties while she worked, hoping this would somehow brighten the cloud darkening her mistress's eyes like a rainbow in a heavy, grey sky, but it seemed to have the opposite effect. The lady's face became more drawn and distant, the beautiful eyes even more troubled, leaving her wondering what could have happened!

Not long after, during the morning assembly, the head servant announced that the commander had contracted a lingering infection. It seemed unbelievable to her that this brave and noble man whom they all revered and feared could be struck down by something as mundane as disease. The weeks following this announcement were full of listless activity but empty of news. They came and went in slow succession. Only the troubling sadness in her Mistress's eyes—a constant reminder that all was not well—remained.

The girl walked thoughtfully across the empty courtyard towards the thick green vegetation over at one corner—a favourite place of refuge whenever she needed to be alone. She mulled over the head servant's last words about the commander: "Our Master has been unwell for some time now, but the king's physician assures me his symptoms are typical of a number of complaints common to us all; however, he is not recovering as quickly as hoped. His strength has been compromised by over exertion from too many campaigns and the pressures of his position as head over all Aram's armies. He needs quiet and rest, so there will be no excess noise or running in the corridors and no congregating to chit-chat in the courtyard. This is an order, and this rule will stay in effect until further notice. If anyone breaks this order then they will be severely punished." Surely if what the head servant said was true, the commander should be getting better, or at least be showing no sign of further deterioration, for that update was over a month ago!

Someone cleared his throat and she looked quickly over in the direction of the sound. Two men, with their heads bent closely in conversation, had entered at the far end of the courtyard. On impulse, she crouched down behind the thick foliage, and, taking care to make no noise, she carefully separated the leaves and peered curiously through the gap that opened. Instantly, she recognized the thick set head and irregular features of the head servant. Ignoring him, she glanced with interest at the stranger. As they came closer, she noted with some alarm that even though the man inclined his ear towards the head servant, his keenly intelligent eyes were avidly scanning the court. With a fast beating heart she slowly let go of most of the leaves until only a fraction of the earlier gap remained. Then the men halted briefly—barely an arm's length away from her. The stranger was talking rapidly, and although his voice was hardly above a whisper, the sound, amplified by the court's quiet stillness, carried clearly.

"... however, what is concerning is that instead of improving he is steadily getting worse. All the previous complaints of dry skin, nose bleeds, and muscle weakness still bother him, but the pain is now more severe. It is still too soon to make any definite diagnosis, and I will need a second opinion before I do, but if what I'm beginning to suspect is true, then, short of a miracle, there is nothing any of us can do. Time alone will tell. Make sure he continues to get plenty of rest. Give him the potions as directed, and hopefully his body will mend and prove me wrong. I will return in a week to see him."

"We will continue to treat him just as you have instructed. I personally see to his medication, and no effort has been spared to insure that the house is quiet so he can rest. But the fact that he is not improving is very worrying ..."

The men moved on and she let out her breath. This was not good news! Whatever could be ailing the man?

Spring quickly matured into summer, and other physicians, besides the king's physician, visited the house, further disrupting the household. Various rumours sprang up and died among the overly suspicious servants. Then the whole establishment was shaken and the mood in the house went from vexed anticipation to brooding sadness as deep sorrow touched the proud family, for leprosy, that dreaded disease, had cast its deadly white shroud upon the commander.

She was devastated. How could such an awful thing happen to the man who had shown her such kindness? Now, besides the physicians, priests—entreating the gods— came and went, but to no avail. All through the tedious months of a hot and dry summer and on to the cooler brilliance of fall, she watched their fruitless prayers and rituals to Baal-Rimmon, the god of war, with concerned interest. When she was a child, her dad often told her stories of the amazing miracles performed by Elijah and Elisha in the name of their God, Yahweh. She was sure that He was the only one who could perform this miracle. But how could she, a mere slave of a despised nation, contest this misplaced trust in these useless gods of theirs and direct the commander to hers?

One wintry-wet morning, some months later, she and another slave were summoned to wash their mistress's hair. The room was deathly quiet. The two girls looked nervously around and saw the lady lying statue-like upon the divan. For a moment, neither was quite sure how to react. They looked helplessly at each other.

The unusual stillness remained throughout the washing, and when they silently dried the long, wet hair. Normally this was one of her most favourite duties, as she loved the feel of the damp and silky strands sliding through her fingers while untangling the tresses with the beautiful jeweled comb. But today the task felt weird. The strange immobility was too upsetting. Suddenly, the mirror wobbled in the hands of the older girl, and she looked up. Her mistress's reflection caught her eye and tore at her young heart. Large tears were spilling out of tightly screwed-up eyes and splashing down crumpled, cotton-white cheeks! Then, before she could stop herself, she blurted out: "If only my Master would see the Prophet who is in Samaria! He would cure him of leprosy."

She held her breath, horrified; the words appallingly loud amid the strained silence. Would she be beaten for her presumption? At first it seemed as though the woman had not heard her and then, as if in a dream, she opened reddened eyes and turned slowly to face her.

"Do you really think so?" she asked mechanically.

"Oh, yes my Lady!" she continued bravely, swallowing hard. "The prophet is famous in Samaria. Once he changed undrinkable water in a spring into fresh, wholesome water. Another time he made a little left over oil in a tiny jar fill so many jars that a widow of one of the prophets could pay her debts. He even raised a dead boy to life!"

Moments passed—moments where it felt as though the woman stared right through her. Then, when she could hardly stand the suspense any longer, her mistress spoke, but so faintly it was hard to catch the words.

"Almost, you give me hope."

Then, frowning slightly, the lady absently twirled the bracelet round her slim, elegant wrist.

"I wonder how true these stories are," she murmured at last, as if to herself. Then, looking the youngster straight in the eye, she asked harshly, "But will this Prophet cure one who is the sworn enemy of his people?"

"Oh my Lady, he can't do anything. It is the Lord God, whom he serves, who has the power to heal my Master!"

"Now you confuse me; first you say it's the Prophet who does these things, and then you tell me it's his god. Which is the truth, or is this merely a trap?"

"Oh Mistress, you mistake me," she cried. "This is no trap, but a genuine desire to see you happy and my Master healed. The prophet is only a servant, even as I am your servant. I do as you bid me do, just as he does what God tells him to do. If God commands him to heal someone who is an enemy of the people, he will not question, but obey."

"Why should your god choose to heal a man who does not worship him?"

"The God of our people is also the creator of all people. He made this world and all that is in it. He and He alone has the power to heal. If my Master were to find the Prophet and request him to ask our God on his behalf, I believe my Master would be healed."

"And why do you believe this so strongly?" she asked, her eyes now alive with curiosity.

"Because my Master saved me!" she answered frankly without thinking. The lady's full lips twitched; she was familiar with the commander's version of the story.

"Perhaps your god judges differently to that of men," she said pensively. A trace of her old sparkle edged the words as she added, "I will tell Naaman what you say, and let him decide what to do."

At first, the girl waited expectantly. Then, when each uneventful day was followed by the next, and her mistress settled once more into indifferent melancholy, she began to believe nothing would happen. But that was not the end of it. Late one afternoon, she was summoned to appear before the commander. The servant led her into a large room shrouded in gloom, and then instantly vanished. She stood uncertainly looking around while her eyes grew accustomed to the diffused light.

"Are you also frightened of me girl?" snarled a deep voice. She jumped with fright.

Gathering her scattered wits, she turned in the direction of the sound. Beside a heavily veiled window lay a shadowy form swathed in loose cloth. She stepped closer and then faltered. Surely this could not be the commander, the great man she knew? That man was a choice man—vibrantly alive, the very essence of a warrior and an exceptional leader! The man she was gazing at appeared insubstantial, hardly recognizable even as a man as he huddled under the covers in the deep gloom. He propped himself up by the elbow.

"Come closer, girl, and take a good look at me. Yes, I see it in your face; I am not the man you remember."

"Sir," she said a little thickly, finding her voice. "You cannot be expected to be anything other than what I find you. You've been issued a death sentence, and that would be hard for anyone, let alone a man like yourself."

At these words his muscles tensed, and with one fluid movement he sat up. "You're either a very brave girl to address your Master in this manner, or a very stupid one! Are you not afraid that I might have you whipped for such insolence?" he spat out harshly.

Her heart gave an uncomfortable lurch at the threat, but she fought the fear, for her words had brought about a subtle transformation in the man. There was now a vague resemblance of the man she admired.

"Sir, the words may appear insolent, but they are the truth. I am not afraid, for I am here at your request to tell you about one who can help you, one who I know can restore your life."

"Come over here, girl, so I can judge whether you are lying or whether you are telling the truth," he barked, while indicating with a concealed hand a spot quite near him.

She came and stood unflinchingly by his side.

"Sit down on the floor, girl, so I can see your eyes," he ordered, the gruff voice now a fraction gentler.

There was a short pause while his hard, desperate eyes searched hers.

"Why would a young Jewish girl forcibly taken from her people and condemned to a life of servitude and slavery want to help me, a man who represents all that has caused her such great pain?" he finally demanded.

"My Lord, it's easy to hate, much harder to forgive," the youngster began tremulously, yet gathering courage as she spoke on. "I have chosen the harder route and have discovered peace in the midst of pain. I have a freedom within that no slavery can destroy. If I have the knowledge of one who can help you, it would be wrong of me to keep that from you, even if you are an enemy!"

He frowned in amazement, saying nothing. The frown deepened and he turned to stare inscrutably at the pale light streaming through the screened window. The silence that followed felt uncomfortable and strange, and she tried not to fidget. Silence, she discovered in that long moment, has a way of loudly demanding its presence be felt. She could hear him breathe slow, deep breaths—considering breaths. At last he turned to face her. Their eyes met—his intent, searching—trying to plumb the depths of her soul, demanding assurance. Then, slowly, the distrust lessened, but the despair remained. Finally, as if satisfied by what he saw, he said quietly, "Yes, I will go and find this prophet. If he is anything like you, perhaps he will call on the name of the Lord your God and heal me."

The last of the winter rains fled before a warmer sun as the commander, in a flurry of frenzied activity, prepared to leave for Samaria with a retinue of men-servants, soldiers, and gifts. Finally the day arrived, and even as the departing convoy of chariots was swallowed up by a ravenous horizon, the tired household settled down to the apprehensive anticipation of his return.

Night after night, during those early and impatient weeks, she praised God, sure that He would honour her trust in him. Then one morning, after pacing around the room restlessly, the lady turned abruptly to face her.

"What will you do if the Master isn't healed? Will you still believe in your god's ability to do miracles?" she snapped. The idle chatter in the room ceased as both the other women turned from their tasks to watch them.

Her mouth dropped open with surprise. This possibility was something she hadn't considered. "He will heal the Master; why shouldn't He? It's an easy thing for Him to do," she said with all the faith and optimism of youth.

"What if he doesn't? Naaman isn't a Jew! Your god is not Naaman's god!"

"My lady, He's healed my pain, and I've asked Him to do this," she answered simply. "God hears us when we speak to him."

"And you think your god will take notice of a measly slave girl?" she almost snarled. At these sharp words the head maid's features pinched together, while a snicker of a smile mirthlessly twisted her companion's hostile face.

"He *will* heal him, my Lady."

The woman was shaken by her gentle assurance. She had never before experienced such faith. Their belief was more a hopeful uncertainty, and it depended entirely on the whim of the god in question. She resumed her pacing, a little furrow puckering her beautiful brow. The girl sat idly watching her, the question revolving over in her mind, and for the first time she experienced some doubt. What if ...? It didn't bare thinking about. She began to pray, but the doubt grew relentlessly as the interminable tap, tap continued. She prayed harder, hating the fear. It felt as though the ground had suddenly shifted, and that nothing was rock stolid.

"Dad,' she cried silently, thoroughly disturbed. "I wish you were here with me. You would tell her that our God is the only God who can heal." As always, the fading image of her father's calm, trusting face renewed her courage. Summoning all her inner strength, she consciously shut out the troubling voice of doubt and the endless tapping of the restless pacing and focused only on the One who had been her constant source of peace over the past months.

Time dragged on, and the slow weeks turned into a couple of months and still no word reached them. Then one hot day, feeling unusually despondent and in a mood for quiet, she made her way quietly down the narrow passage to the dorm she shared with the other women slaves. If she was lucky, it would be empty and she would have a few precious and much needed moments alone. The entrance was in sight when she paused briefly

74

to flick away an irksome fly that kept settling on her head. An irritated but instantly recognizable voice wafted through the open doorway.

"Who does she think she is, the Queen of Sheba? Sending the Master on some wild goose chase and getting the mistress's hopes up all for nothing?"

It was clear to the girl standing out in the passage that only she could be the person to whom the woman was referring. Colour swept into her cheeks at this gross misrepresentation of her motives. In the turmoil of the moment she stood irresolute, not sure whether to go in and defend herself or just quietly walk away.

"This is not the way to ingratiate herself with them. When the master returns unhealed she will be severely whipped for this folly." She froze, for this speaker was none other than the head maid.

"That's all very well if she is the only one who is punished, but we might all suffer because of what she has done, and that's not fair!" answered a sullen voice, which she instantly recognized as belonging to the older girl who shared her duties. She gasped at this betrayal of their friendship.

"Well, if her high and mighty ideas do bring their wrath on us all, then we will make sure she gets what's coming to her," smugly tittered the first woman. "We'll teach her to never try a trick like this ever again!"

The hurtful words, with their hidden threats, cut deep. Tears stung her eyes and with a torn look on her face, she whirled about and fled. She rushed back to the courtyard and looked urgently around. Thankfully no-one was in sight and she made for her secret spot—her hidden sanctuary. Safe at last, the torrent she could no longer hold back poured down. How could they think this of her? How could they even imagine this was her motive?

After this incident she became an outsider. None of the women swapped funny stories with her anymore. Instead she bore the brunt of their anger through many caustic comments while the men just distanced themselves from the one they feared might bring wrath upon them all. Loneliness, that foreign companion of earlier days, came back to pay another lengthy visit.

Another month rolled by without word, and the tension in the house reached fever pitch. Then, late one morning, the pressure, like a dam bursting its banks, broke at the sound of horns blowing in the distance. Immediately, everyone streamed out the rooms, through the grand entranceway, and on down the sweeping staircase to the road. A cloud of dust clearly visible in the distance heralded the long awaited return of the commander and his retinue.

The young slave hesitated at the top of the marble stairs, feeling something akin to panic as she stared down at all the other servants and slaves clustered anxiously around their mistress on the flagstone paving below. The lady was standing erect and still, staring fixedly at the slowly advancing vehicles. Only her hands, continually clasping and unclasping, betrayed her agitated excitement. The girl watched her for a moment but could not bring herself to go down and join the gathering. Then she tensed, for coldly curious glances had sought and found her standing alone under the archway above. She quailed under this new onslaught, shielding her eyes from their icy stares with a hand that shivered like a leaf in a constant draft.

The moment of reckoning had finally come.

After some agonizing minutes the foremost chariot came clearly into view and the driver slowed the horses down to an even trot. Her heart sank at this action, for surely if there was a miracle to report they would arrive in a frenzy of excitement. Suddenly nothing made sense—everything felt wrong! Are the slaves right? Has it been folly to be so sure? The questions tore at her wavering faith. Involuntarily, her eyes slid again to the group below and caught the disgusted glare of her adversary. Reeling from the blatant loathing she stepped backwards as if struck by a blow.

Utterly unnerved, she looked back at the halting car. She found its only other occupant. Then her vision blurred and she crumpled against the wall, grasping the stone behind her for support. Unquestionably the man was still wrapped in the all-concealing cloak he had worn on the day of his departure!

The head-servant leapt down off his perch, his face expressionless as he waited patiently for his master to descend. The commander, his head covered over by a deep hood, grasped the metal frame for support and pulled himself up like an old man. Their mistress stood pale and still as the frozen moon, her mouth half open with shock. Then she gave a little cry and rushed forward in eager distress, blithely disregarding the dangers of disease. A barely audible cry escaped the girl's colourless lips, and the last vestige of her faith wilted, like a flower that's been severed from its life-giving stem, under the crushing censure that rose from the throng of servants keeping a respectful and wary distance.

Suddenly the commander, with a flourish, threw off the heavy cloak and sprang down to the ground. With a happy shout he grabbed his wife by the waist and swung her high in the air. For an instant the watching crowd stood shocked and uncertain, like a herd of deer before they turn and flee, and then an exuberant cheer burst forth even as she sagged like a sack of grain to the floor, sobbing weakly. God had not failed her!

Over the following days, she was filled with awe and wonder as it became apparent to the entire household that the only God the commander would now serve and honour was hers!

Food for Thought

I felt like I was the only one oppressed by a dark cloud as I stared down at the cosmopolitan throng buzzing contentedly about the colourful stalls under a brilliant summer sky of flawless blue. I had no time to waste and, thoroughly disgruntled, I grumbled aloud, "Where have all these people come from? The market is not usually this crowded. It's going to take much longer to get through all my shopping today."

The path downwards was not too steep, and soon I was one with the swarming horde. I gazed distractedly around at the seemingly endless variety of delectable wares scattered like piles of discarded washing on every available surface. Fresh loaves of bread, dried fish, scarlet and purple silks, rolls of indigo blue cloth, and richly dyed woven carpets dazzled my eyes. Baskets overflowing with bright red tomatoes, boldly orange pumpkins, glossy yellow peppers, fresh green cucumbers, and purple-blue aubergines splashed an enticing rainbow of colour, gaily mocking this jaded mood of mine. Only the subdued black olives, pressed too tightly together, empathized with me. Whichever way I looked, thick knots of people were eagerly demanding service from equally voluble and obliging venders. Over to my left stood a row of large clay tubs filled to the brim with the morning's catch of fresh pink lobster and these too had just as long line-ups.

The local Tyre fishermen must be delighted with this crowd, but it's a feeling not shared by their haul, I thought pityingly as I glanced at the squeaking crustaceans frantically crawling over one another in their futile but desperate attempt to escape the unnatural confinement. Then my mercenary taste buds kicked into action and I abandoned their cause and stood at the back of the line waiting my turn to grab one.

Still, the lobsters' predicament had had some effect, and I stood pondering the similarities between their dilemma and my own. Their torment was obvious to one and all and would soon be over, unlike that of my daughter's. Her suffering would be life-long. And now her father was making it even harder! Just yesterday we'd argued heatedly about her going out in public. I could understand not taking her with me when she wasn't quite herself, like today. But to want to keep her housebound out of fear of a possible incident was simply wrong! He was being quite unreasonable, for these attacks weren't every day. Surely people would understand if something unusual were to happen.

I surveyed the happy crowd with a new measure of cynicism. What abnormal family secrets did they hide behind the friendly masks they wore?

A couple of sales were successfully concluded, and I gratefully shuffled forward. I recognized the voice of the lady now being served. She was quite the chatterbox. As I listened to their chit-chat, I hoped the vender wouldn't be drawn into a lengthy conversation. Even if the lineup continued to move at its present rate, it was going to take far longer than I cared to wait.

I turned my thoughts away from the sales transacting at the front of the lineup and back to my daughter. What was the matter with her today? Was she perhaps catching a cold? Or was it something worse? No, it couldn't be that; it's too soon since the last attack! I discarded the disturbing thought as one shakes off an unwanted touch. I really shouldn't worry so, I chided myself sharply, but I knew full well that it was a waste of time.

"No, I cannot give into fear every time she frets, I just cannot!" Unconsciously I spoke aloud in Greek.

"So, what's happened to the little lass then?" asked a thin, wheezy voice at my elbow. Startled, I swung around and almost knocked over an ancient, leaning on his knobbed walking stick.

"Oh, she's not feeling too well, so I left her in Zadora and Thomas's care. It's probably nothing serious," I said casually ... too casually. "She's most likely just getting a cold. It's that time of year."

"Eh, that's too bad! She's like a flower that one; always has a welcome smile for an old man. Makes me forget my aches and pains! Don't you go and worry your pretty head too much about her, now; she's young yet and she'll quickly get over whatever it is, just you wait and see. In a few days she'll be her own sweet self again," comforted the old sage, his shrewd eyes missing nothing.

"Thanks, I'll try not to," I mumbled politely, smiling into the faded blue eyes surrounded by their sea of creases, and feeling some of the pent-up tension ease a little.

He's only trying to be kind, I thought, watching the old Phoenician hobble away. He doesn't understand what lies behind my concern. He just assumes that she's like all the other children. Mindful again of a need for haste, I glared impatiently at the dealer, only to realize that he *was* caught up in animated discussion. Some mutual cousin by the sounds of things and, judging by the varied expressions of amusement on the other customers faces, no-one seemed to mind the hold-up. If anything, they were delighted to hear the tale of this miscreant's mischief. Under normal circumstances, I probably would have too.

Biting back an apt but unfavorable remark, I wondered whether to hang on or go and find a stall where I could get faster service. At that moment the story, amid bursts of laughter, ended. Then the woman, realizing she had an audience, started off on another long yarn, and that settled the issue.

"She's definitely in fine form," I muttered under my breath as I pushed my way through the milling throng, anxiously searching for any break in the lengthy line-ups. There were none. The only spot that appeared to be less busy was near a cluster of pistachio trees on the farthest side of the market. This was where a collection of kosher stalls stood, whose merchandise was strictly tailored for Jews. I hovered uncertainly, indecisively, before them. "I really would prefer a wider selection, but these stalls aren't so busy. I can get most of what I need here. The other groceries will have to wait for another day. But it will have to be fish and not lobster for us today," I murmured ruefully. Realizing that this dithering was wasting even more time, I walked quickly over to the nearest fish cart, debating whether to buy tuna or bream.

I heard only the occasional Arabic phrase outside their traditional tongue as I waited. Soon I was face to face with the elderly dealer. For an instant I wondered if there would be a language barrier, for I knew little Hebrew, and I doubted whether he could speak Greek. But I needn't have worried, for he addressed me in fluent Arabic. Finally, after some heated bartering, both of us were satisfied and coins and fish exchanged hands.

It is possible that, because my nerves were already a little jangled and I was feeling more sensitive than usual, that this is why I began to notice a subtle difference in manner whenever I was served. The notion of bias was hard to pin down to a single incident. Nothing stood out; there was no comment or action that was either rude or out of place to justify the feeling, yet the idea of being "less than" persisted. Perhaps it was the offhand indifference to me as a person, coupled with a cooler tone of voice that communicated the slight discrimination so effectively. I'm a fairly liberal Grecian, and this attitude was irritating. Keeping my responses deliberately neutral, I fought back a pert remark.

"I wonder why they respond in this manner," I muttered, annoyed. "Is it because I'm a woman, or is it because they believe that they are a cut above the rest?"

The crowd began to thin, and I made good progress. Still short of oranges, I strode over to a fruit stand nestled under the fringe of a long line of nut trees. I selected a couple from an almost empty basket, and then looked around for assistance. I was mildly amused to see the attention of the young attendant fixed on an attractive girl with cheeks as rosily red as the apples she was inspecting in a tub nearby. I watched them for a moment. Then, as I turned away, I glimpsed the broad back of a man slipping behind the thick, leafy foliage into the dark shadows beyond.

Just then a Jewish merchant, a neighbor of mine, moved cautiously toward the same spot. There was something secretive about his manner that was intriguing. I shifted position to get a better view. The loiterer stepped out of the deep shade and the two exchanged quick greetings in their native tongue. This man was younger and stronger than the bony merchant and had the bearing of one familiar with the outdoors. Judging by his clothes, he was most likely a fisherman, but no ordinary fisherman. Even at this distance there was something fascinating about him that I couldn't quite put my finger on.

The young vender coughed politely, and I spun to face him. Instantly I enquired the price and bought more oranges than I needed. Then another customer claimed his attention, so I moved quickly away to the now vacant position in front of the inviting apples and set down the heavy basket. Here, surprisingly, I had an even better view of the young fisherman. His face, close-up, was strong and open, and frankly contradicted his present reserve. He had a distinct air of authority about him, which his humble apparel in no sense diminished. I know I was gaping at him, when his vibrantly alive eyes caught mine. My cheeks instantly burned. Somehow, in a way I couldn't understand, that pure stare made me feel exactly like a robber caught red-handed in the act.

Feeling like a fool, I quickly selected an apple. *Perhaps some Jews are different*, I conceded grudgingly to this inanimate spectator of my humiliation. Still feeling the searing authenticity of those remarkable and compelling eyes, and not wanting to be caught staring again, I grabbed more apples and twisted around to find the vender. Suddenly, a sneering voice in fluent Aramaic cut across the breeze.

"Greetings, friends, has the son of David arrived yet?"

Startled, I looked back over my shoulder. A different Jew, a man whom I disliked, was rapidly approaching the two men. *How does he fit in this interesting puzzle?* I wondered grimly, now deliberately stalling. From under my eyelashes I watched him surreptitiously.

The two men froze, and I was struck by their expressions as they glanced at each other. Then the merchant mumbled something inaudible to the fisherman before turning to glare at the newcomer.

Undaunted, Zabad said insolently, "The Rabbi wants to know how long the teacher intends to stay, and if there is still a meeting planned for tonight?"

There was a quick pause and another exchange of glances before the thick-set fisherman reluctantly replied in heavily accented Aramaic. "He won't stay long; he never does."

The merchant took firm hold of the fisherman's arm, mumbled some excuse, and the two men moved off, leaving the intruder standing irresolute and alone.

"So, someone important is coming and those two don't want this to get around," I whispered discreetly in Greek to the uninterested apples. "I wonder who this "son of David" can be."

Zabad stared thoughtfully at the ground, his mouth twisting unpleasantly, and then, looking up, he caught sight of me. He smiled contemptuously. I stared coolly back. His eyes glinted and then narrowed. He strolled over, even as the youthful assistant came up.

"Only dogs with no breeding have the presumption to stray into the kennels of pedigrees!" he remarked casually to the young man hovering at my elbow, before spitting insultingly on the ground.

My cheeks instantly flared. *What a detestable man you are! This disgusting comment does not deserve an answer*, I raged inwardly, choking back a thoroughly undignified retort. Jabad laughed unpleasantly. I glared up at him, wishing I could slap him. Still laughing, he spun on his axis, and with a distinct swagger in his gait, left us. I breathed long and deep as I watched him go, my outrage dissolving into impotent frustration at my limitations as a woman. *My husband always said my face betrays the true me*, I thought bitterly, as my colour settled, for having given him the satisfaction of knowing that his barb had hit home. The young attendant fiddled awkwardly with a few apples and then began to arrange and then rearrange the scarlet fruit as the silence stretched.

The blushing witnesses of this offensive insult refused to stack in any orderly fashion, and their rebellion was strangely comforting. Finally, the youth gained the upper hand and, turning his head fractionally, stared pointedly from under surprisingly long lashes at the apples still clutched in my hands. When I did not respond, those girlish eyes appraised me with an unmistakable gleam that made me feel hot all over again, even as his unemployed fingers began to twist his long ear locks. Utterly provoked, I deliberately dropped the apples in my hands onto the precarious arrangement, toppling the pile over. I grabbed my basket, gave him a quick dismissive nod, and stalked off, my thoughts in a furious turmoil.

"How *dare* Zabad insult me like that; how *dare* he infer that I am nothing more than a common dog, and that he is so much superior! What a horrid nobody. What right has he to speak about me like this before that precocious young man?" I stormed.

The boiling emotions took a while before they simmered and settled, and for once I was grateful for the long walk home. It was with a lighter step that I eventually rounded the last bend in the road.

The house was now clearly visible and Thomas, seeing me, came running up the deserted lane. "Mistress, come quickly, your daughter is having another attack," he yelled.

"Oh no, not that! Anything but that! It can't be that, it can't, and so soon on the heels of the other!" I cried, inwardly berating myself for having so completely forgotten her.

"How long has it been going on for?" I yelled back.

"Not long, Mistress," he shouted, distraught. And then, upon reaching me, he said between pants. "I caught her as she fell, so she didn't hurt herself this time. Zadora is with her now."

I threw him the laden basket and ran the last stretch to the house, yanking the door open, and fell, gasping for breath, beside her floppy little body jerking and twitching hideously on the floor. A chill ran down my spine; these new spasms were the worst so far.

"It's bad, Zadora, it's really bad!" I whimpered, on the verge of hysteria.

"No, Mistress, don't say so. You need to calm yourself; she will get better!"

"She must; she must!" I cried somewhat incoherently. Then, before I could stop myself, I wailed, "But what if she doesn't? What if one day she doesn't and I lose her forever?"

When the fit was finally over, I gathered her tightly to me and crooned softly between choked-back sobs. "It's okay, darling, Mummy's here. It's okay; don't worry, you can rest now. Mummy's here."

Zadora fussed over us for a while and then, finally satisfied that we were both alright, left to join Thomas in the kitchen. The day was well advanced and there was still much to be done before starting the evening meal.

I gazed at the worn little face as the long black lashes slowly drooped shut, covering sweet trusting eyes, and involuntarily shuddered! Here were no rosily flushed cheeks, warm with the dew of life; instead, they were deathly pale. How I hated these dreadful attacks! They were slowly but surely destroying this precious life. If only there was a way to free her of them!

There must be some way. There has to be; I can't lose her, I thought over and over, caught up in a black despair, feeling the intolerable burden of these fits anew as I stared at her exhausted little face. Then, randomly, the snippet of conversation I'd heard earlier that morning popped back into my mind. It's amazing how in the midst of dark trauma a part of our minds will be busy sorting out some puzzle that has little or no connection with the immediate crisis. So it was with me now, and somehow I'd made the connection, without any consciousness of how or why, that this man, this son of David, was the prophet who was said to have performed some amazing miracles.

News of these miracles had spread quickly throughout the surrounding area and become the hot topic of conversation in the town. The Tyre elders debated daily among themselves whether he was the long-awaited Messiah of the Jews, who was to be born of the line of David.

"What if this man really is the Messiah? What if he really is him?" I whispered yearningly as I sat, feeling the steady beat of her heart beat hope into mine.

"If only I could somehow find a way to get close to him—close enough to ask him if he would be willing to help you get better," I murmured, unexpectedly aware of a peculiar sense of loss and an equally strange longing for something, which at that moment I could not even begin to express.

"If these stories are true, then this prophet *has* to represent the real God, the creator of everything!" I exclaimed softly. I could readily believe that anyone who fed and healed thousands of people, even bringing the dead back to life, could only be from God. I stood up, suddenly alive with anticipation, and carried the sleeping child over to her bed and laid her down. Immediately, my thoughts darkened.

"Why should he help me?" I muttered. "After all, I am not a Jew, not one of God's *special* people. I'm nothing more than a heathen dog in their eyes!" Anger surged and embraced not just the provoker of that insult, but the whole nation, as the spiteful words stabbed deeper into the raw wound. Thoroughly agitated, I quietly paced the room.

And then the brilliant purity shining out from the stranger's eyes looked across space and time at me. A chill ran down my spine. *These thoughts are getting me nowhere fast. I am becoming like Zabad! Even if I can approach this son of David, how can I even think of doing so if I feel this resentful? What right do I, as a heathen, have to demand my daughter's healing from one so much greater and more powerful than this simple fisherman, from one whom God has sent to heal His people?*

A terrible heaviness weighed down on me, and I sank before my daughter's softly sleeping form.

"I am a heathen and full of really bad attitudes, but this man, if he *is* the prophet, has the power to heal you." I sobbed into the bedspread. This fresh gush of tears had a wonderful cleansing effect and soon I felt lighter. My daughter moaned softly and thrashed about restlessly under the loose coverlet, her eyes half open. I froze, the weeping instantly checked. I watched her anxiously, but nothing further happened. Her eyelids slowly drooped and closed, like shutters over a window, as she settled back into restful sleep. I frowned as I remembered those amazing miracles. "If only I was a Jew, I could openly plead my case. Oh, if only there was a way to tell him about you!" I muttered again in frustration, still buckling against my husband's restraints of having to keep our predicament so secret.

Snippets of the conversation I'd overheard that morning returned to plague me until, at last, they made sense—rather like the way random puzzle pieces slowly converge to form a picture. "I *can* find him!" I announced a little crazily to the hushed room. "There's to be a meeting this evening! I bet he is the merchant's guest while he is here. So what if I'm not a Jew, and not invited? The door of opportunity will always open to those brave enough to knock! If their God is the creator of us all, then he made me, too; all I can do is ask, and the worst he can do is refuse."

Suddenly I panicked, for now the impossible had become possible. *If I actually find him, what will I do if he refuses me and she isn't healed? What then? There will be no more hiding our little girl's problem. Everyone will know about it, and what will my husband do when he finds out? And if I do enter our neighbor's home uninvited, I could offend not just Jabad, but all the Jews' sensibilities, and they will never forgive an insult like that. They will shun us and blame my husband for my indiscretion.* I paced the room on pitiably weak feet of clay as I wrestled with these thoughts, thinking through all the implications for us and for our family.

With a flash of insight I cried softly, "That's it! That's what's really holding me back—my own pride and fear! So much for my bravado. What a hypocrite I am! I am really no different from my husband. When the trimming is removed, I'm cut from the same cloth!" I sighed heavily. This was yet another moment of truth in a day which seemed set to shatter what was left of my fragile ego.

"If only you knew what a coward your mother really is. Now that a door has opened, I don't know if I have the courage to go through it!" I whispered sadly to her loveable slumbering little face.

But what if you die because I was too scared? How then will I live with myself? If I don't try to find him, I will never know if you might have been healed. *I have to try, even if I fail. I have to.* These thoughts ignited a new determination.

"Yes," I deliberated quietly, feeling like a timid young child about to climb a dauntingly tall tree to rescue a pet kitten. "Even if he refuses to heal you, I have to try—for your sake; for my sake."

I sat down on the bed and gently caressed her hair. "So what do I have to lose by doing this?" I continued quietly. "Just my fear and appalling pride, and that's not that much after all, darling. I have to try! I have to find him; I have to! The fisherman said he won't stay long. *What if he has left already?*"

Galvanized by a strong sense of urgency, I jumped quickly to my feet. "Thomas, Zadora! There you are! Please keep an eye on my daughter. I'm going out and may not be back for some time. Save me some supper; I'll eat it when I return."

Feeling as if each minute lost was robbing me of this one and only chance, I grabbed my cloak, pulling it over me as I headed off in the direction of the merchant's house. I could only hope that my hunch was correct and that the prophet was staying at his house.

"Please, God of the Jews," I prayed as I hurried along, "let me find the son of David!" Then a new question, challenging and wonderful in its novelty, lit my thinking.

"Yes," I whispered recklessly in answer to the unspoken question." If You let me come face to face with the Jews' Messiah, I will swallow my pride and bow down to him before them all, even that vile Zabad. I will even admit they are God's chosen people if this is what it takes to heal her. I will do anything for her—anything!"

I turned the last corner. Over to one side stood the prestigious home with an unusually large group of men and women crowding the doorway.

"He's here!" I cried and, before anyone knew what I was about, I'd pushed my way past these bystanders and brazenly entered the home. My sole aim was to find the fisherman. I was sure that if I found him I would find the Prophet. It was my best and only plan!

Once inside I stopped abruptly. I blinked rapidly to adjust my eyes to the dim light. The room was tightly packed with people crowded together in a circle, some sitting and others standing. Everywhere were faces— shocked faces!

I sucked in my breath, for judging from the frigid anger glaring at me, I only had a few moments before I was thrown out! I stared wildly around, instantly recognizing the owners of the house and then recoiling from Zabad's livid face. Then I saw the fisherman. There was no mistake; his intense eyes bore briefly into mine before fixing on the man sitting beside him. I looked in the same direction and found a rather nondescript face which appeared lost in thought. Stunned, I gaped at him for a few agonizing seconds. Surely *this* couldn't be the son of David, the future king of the Jews. So where was he? *Which one was he?*

There was movement ... noises behind me ... noises beside me; any moment now a hand might grab me. I had to find him; I had to! And quickly!

Again I looked at the puzzled face of the fisherman, grasping for reassurance, willing him to point me in the right direction. He in turn swung around to look questioningly at the man alongside him.

"Are you he?" I cried inwardly as I, following his example, found myself being quietly watched.

Then our eyes met! Casting caution and pride to the wind, I shouted, "Have mercy, please have mercy! My daughter is suffering terribly from demon-possession. Oh please, please have mercy!"

The man looked entirely unperturbed.

Dismayed, I stared at him, frantically wringing my hands and pleading. "Lord, please heal my daughter; have mercy on me!"

An uproar erupted behind me. Voices—loud voices— were clamouring for attention. Fearing imminent eviction, I stepped quickly, recklessly, forward.

"Lord, *Son of David*, have mercy on me!" I yelled at full volume, my whole being beseeching, acknowledging his divine ability.

Ignoring all our cries, the man calmly studied us. Jabad's imperious voice rose above the noisy censure, urging him to send me away. He still didn't speak. Instead, now it felt to me as though, for him, we had all ceased to exist and that he was, if this impression was true, quietly listening to another. That strange, inexpressible calm that clung like a robe about the man began to affect me, to settle me.

Encouraged, I begged again, "Lord, Son of David, have mercy on me. My daughter is suffering terribly."

His thoughtful expression deepened and then he regarded me again. I shivered, for I had never before felt so *seen*. He raised his hand, and immediately the clamour stilled.

"I was sent only to the lost sheep of Israel," he said at last.

"Lord, have mercy on me; please set her free!" I cried and threw myself down before him, my voice painfully desperate.

Silence! Nothing but silence! Except for the rapid and expectant breathing, the whole room was still; not a hand moved, not a foot shifted.

"Lord, help me!" I begged with hands outstretched, my voice choking up and sounding painfully small amid the disconcerting quiet.

He glanced about the room before turning to me with just the smallest hint of a smile in his eyes. "First let the children eat all they want, for it is not right to take the children's bread and toss it to their dogs," he replied deliberately, watchfully.

Some snickered unpleasantly at this. Glancing sideways I caught a glimpse of Jabad's smirking face.

"Yes, Lord, but even the dogs eat the crumbs that fall from their masters' tables." I said without hesitation.

"Woman, you have great faith! For such a reply you may go; your request is granted." His words wiped away Jabad's vile expression as effectively as a cloth mops up a messy spill. I floated, as if on a cloud, all the way home to find my rosy-cheeked daughter relaxed on the bed, the torment gone for good.

The Garment

"The Spirit of the sovereign Lord is on me, because the Lord has anointed
me to preach good news to the poor. He has sent me to bind up the broken-
hearted, to proclaim freedom for the captives and release from darkness for
the prisoners ... to comfort all who mourn, and provide for those who grieve
in Zion—to bestow on them a crown of beauty instead of ashes, the oil of joy
instead of mourning, and a garment of praise instead of a spirit of despair."
—Isaiah 61:1–3

Dark clouds blazed with streaks of flamboyant red and gold as the
swift chariots of dawn burnt a fiery trail of light through the deep
shadows of the turbulent heavens above. I leaned further out the window
to get a better view of the spectacular drama spanning the skies and shivered as a sudden blast of cold hit my face. The old-time saying of red skies
in the morning bringing a warning of rain is true, I thought, as I eyed the
ominously glowing heavens. The day ahead is sure to be stormy!

Slowly the spectacular display evolved into the ordinary, so I stumbled away from the window back to the welcome warmth of the bed and
my lover still wrapped in slumberous shadow. Perhaps now I would be able
to fall into that deep and restful sleep that had eluded me all night. Pleas-
antly chilled, I snuggled close against his body and wearily shut my eyes.

But that wish was not to be, and a tiresome headache began to work
its way from temple to temple. The atmosphere inside the small, stuffy
room grew steadily muggier as I tossed and turned under the too warm
bedding. Finally I abandoned the useless attempt to sleep and opened dry,
burning eyes. The air smelt unbearably stale, my throat felt parched, and
the covers were uncomfortably hot and itchy. I shifted upright and allotted
the offending blanket to the realm of my feet with one quick shove, relish-
ing the feeling of being instantly cooler, even as the sharp pain between my
eyes began to fade.

I looked down at the tranquil, slumbering body of the man next to
me. The slow, rhythmic breathing moved his chest up and down, and my

tired gaze lifted and dropped with each breath. Fascinated, I sat watching for a while longer, empty of all conscious thought. Then I stared absently into space, just feeling feelings, as the light steadily gained strength. Slowly the pain from stiffening, stationary muscles disrupted the restful emptiness, bringing me unwillingly to an aching awareness of the present.

I changed position, taking in with one sweeping glance the depressing dinginess of the furnishings—the cracked and stained mirror; the blackened and spattered candle stubs on their lusterless metal stands, robbed now of the dreamy glow of their former glory; the dregs of cheap wine discoloring the bottoms of the empty tumblers. All the alluring warmth of romance dispelled in an instant to morbid shabbiness that resonated with the foul taste in my mouth.

I reached over and tentatively touched my lover, wanting to arouse him from a distant dreamland and needing his sure caress to chase away the troubling disquiet. But he turned over, presenting to me instead his cold and comfortless back. I closed my dampened eyes tightly, shutting out the room, shutting in the pain, hearing only the contented breathing, just inches apart and yet an eternity away.

A mad desire to shake him awake, to make him actually *look* at me, to acknowledge the real me and see my need, filled me. Instead, I gripped the edge of the bed. Gradually the longing lessened and feeling like trash, I slid slowly off the bed.

"How is it possible to sleep without an apparent care in the world?" I grumbled resentfully under my breath. I staggered over to where my clothes lay rumpled and scattered on the chair and clutched at the bundle like one drowning. I fought an unrealistic yearning to live life over, to make different choices. How fleeting the adolescent years; those years where, unbeknown to many of us, we choose the direction that sets our path in stone, yet at that time they felt to me like they would last forever.

"Even if I could go back to that point in time, would it be any different? Could I change? Would I do anything differently, or would I be just as restless, just as quick to chase after the first bit of excitement that offered an easy escape?" I asked myself. After some moments of reflection, I decided no—no, I wouldn't be any different.

"What's the matter with me today? Even if I tried I can't change the past, it is what it is!" I muttered firmly and angrily as I roughly shook out the fresh creases on the clothing inflicted by yesterday's wearing. Feeling profoundly disturbed, I took my time to dress.

That boredom had been fatal, a trap set to go off … and then I met the boy—the boy with too bold an eye and a reckless charm who traversed enticing and forbidden paths, paths which I was only too ready to venture on. Always the wild dreamer, he made such an impression with his daring words. Hopelessly, helplessly captivated, I hadn't seen the danger of that empty talk, which melted away into thin air like smoke. I was too naïve! How ironic that we met at a wedding; it should have been a funeral. This was where I took my first unguarded step on that downward spiral that quickly leads to the death of one's innocence. I gazed at nothing in particular for a few minutes.

How completely he won my trust. That meeting was only the beginning of many meetings, secret meetings, where I gave myself willingly and foolishly to him. Then suddenly I was pregnant. My brave hero couldn't take the heat, and like mist under the morning sun evaporated from sight. Strange that I should think of him now. I haven't thought about him for years. I wonder where he is, or if he ever thinks about our child or cares what became of him. My thoughts switched to the man chosen by my parents; how very different he was to my lover. He hadn't questioned my compliance or the speed of our marriage, or how quickly I fell pregnant. How proud he was the day *his* son was born!

"Fallen" was the ideal word to describe my condition, for I had indeed fallen, but my husband was too trusting to understand just how far, I thought cynically, as I quietly tidied the room. *If only that was the full extent of my madness!* But it was only the beginning of the lies, the endless, sordid lies that trapped and held me fast in a sticky, sickening web of deceit. Why did I treat the only man who genuinely loved me so badly? I struggled vainly to understand the underlying motive. Was it just boredom, or was it that I never really loved him? Or was it the fact that I had a lover? Truly God is right when He states that the heart is deceitful above all things and beyond cure. For who indeed can understand it? I cringed, hating the hindsight. Sighing heavily, I picked up the cracked mirror.

"You're an appalling mess!" I informed my one-dimensional twin snappily. Her flawed face stared stormily back in agreement. I looked quickly away from the truth glaring at me through those accusing eyes.

"Time is the only teacher, and her lessons for the wayward are hard!" I whispered despondently, and then, turning back to face the mirror, growled. "And this is more than enough reminiscing!" The mute image nodded willingly enough, but my conscience refused to pay attention, being bent on its own course of misery.

All went well until I met *him*. His face stood out in the crowded room, and it was as though no-one else existed. With the brilliant strokes of a master, his portrait was firmly painted in my mind, and his image haunted me until I felt as though I were going mad. If only I had run away that day, as far away as I could get from him, I might have been able to withstand the overpowering feelings. Instead, I gave in to the burning emotions and shamelessly encouraged a relationship. At first it felt like heaven; there were sweet stolen moments and clandestine rendezvous until, inevitably, we were found out. How foolish I was. Had I really believed we wouldn't be? I scowled at the fractured reflection as the fine-toothed comb tore violently at wild tresses. What insanity had possessed me to throw everything to the wind?

Long repressed images came sharply, painfully into focus. My husband's hurt and disbelieving eyes, and the children's tense, white little faces scorched my soul, and I folded my arms tightly to still their empty longing for the children. To think he was even prepared to forgive me! Oh, the madness of that moment when I left the substance for the fantasy; he disowned me then! Was it only yesterday when I bumped into my son and he ignored me, pretending he hadn't seen me, while trying to hide that give-away expression of despising humiliation?

"I know that look all too well, but it still hurts so much!" I muttered, wiping my wet eyes. Oh, the cruel fickleness of foolish feelings; the cost was too great, and the returns too little!

"Stop crying, woman, you earned all this!" I whispered furiously to the forlorn face staring miserably back at me from the mirror as I slowly bound the last defiant strand of hair into place. "Don't kid yourself; you wouldn't have listened to anyone, not even the voice of an angel!"

The rain pelted down hard and loud overhead. I moved slowly over to the window and lent heavily against the wood casing. The sky was shrouded over in dark, unpenetrable cloud. Short, staccato bursts of wind relentlessly whipped the bent and drenched branches of the vulnerable trees into submission. For a long while I watched the unmerciful beating, feeling utterly beaten myself. With limp fingers I pulled a stray hair off my tongue. Everything I did felt like an effort, and I shivered. It *couldn't* be happening again; this couldn't be the beginning of one of *those* moments! The haunting recollection of the seemingly endless moments of black despair chased away all other thought as the dread intensified.

"I *have* to stop thinking of the past and remain in the present. It *must* be that unexpected interaction with my son that is bringing back all this morbid nostalgia," I whispered wildly, desperately willing the man snoring quietly on the bed to wake-up.

He stirred and yawned; I watched hopefully, expectantly. Instead of awakening, however, he settled down into a more comfortable position. Even as I bit back the deep disappointment, I knew that any hope for reassurance was futile; he wasn't the sensitive and caring type, nor was he able to handle any flood of emotional passion. Guilt and tears and self-recrimination only annoyed and left him coldly withdrawn. The best I could hope for was detached companionship, so generally I suppressed all desire for more than this.

A few minutes passed while I chewed my lip uneasily. What if one day I couldn't shake off this ominous mood, what then? If only I had a friend to turn to instead of an endless stream of lovers—someone who really cared. Then I wouldn't be quite so lonely.

"Why can't you be kinder, sweeter?" I demanded silently, urgently to the inert form, and then I fought another unreasonable desire to shake him awake to answer me. Suddenly, the earlier longing to start over, to begin again with a fresh slate, came achingly back.

"Why do I need you so much, why am I so weak?" I cried mutely. If only I had the strength to leave this way of life and start again. Oh, if only there really was a way to start over. There has to be a way, my heart cried, there has to be! Maybe someday I will go away, far away, and really begin again. Even as this noble thought resonated with my soul, passionate memories of the night before gripped and filled me with sickening desire, and I knew with a sinking heart that I was truly trapped. I could not change! I was nothing less than a shuddering slave to the deviant demands of lust. It was all an empty wish.

The cool, moist air was laden with scented freshness. Common narcissus nestled in clumps along the edges of the small black-basalt stone dwellings, their rain-battered faces welcomed the pale sunshine bravely breaking through the cloud. It was already mid-morning, and besides the usual plaintiff bark or cheep of a hen and child's cry, the street was unusually quiet for so late an hour. Both the unexpected quiet and the damp beauty about me were immensely comforting, and I was grateful for the long walk down the winding road. The market where I was headed was situated about a mile past the bend which housed the large ornate synagogue. Soon the clean white-washed stone facing that sprawling building became visible.

An animated hum, the first real noise I'd heard since leaving the tiny apartment, met me when I rounded the corner. A large knot of people were pressed tightly together in front of the wide shallow stairs, and for once no one noticed me. Some were calling out the name "Jesus," while others cried out to be healed. Puzzled but curious, I walked warily forward. I halted a few paces behind those on the periphery, even as a rich, vibrant voice rose up, clear of the clamour. I pushed a little closer to see, craning over the necks immediately in front, but try as I might, I could not glimpse the man holding our attention.

"For God so loved the world that He gave His one and only son, that whoever believes in him shall not perish, but have everlasting life. For God did not send His son into the world to condemn the world, but to save the world through him."

"This isn't for me; I'm too much of a sinner. I don't deserve God's love," I murmured as the meaning hit home. I hastily turned around, but the words settled and stuck like dew-dampened seeds sprouting tiny shoots of hope.

Who is this son of God anyway? I wondered, hesitating.

I looked back over my shoulder. Somehow, by some freak in the laws of possibility, a gap opened up, and there sitting in full view on the rain-splashed stairs was the man, pitching his persuasive and compelling words. I stared up at him. Who *is* he? Is he talking about himself? Can *he* be this son of God? Our eyes locked, and I had the strangest impression that all my innermost private thoughts and feelings were an open book to him. The moment stretched on, but still those challenging and probing and sympathetic eyes held mine. In that moment, every lie I'd chosen to believe was uncovered for the sin it was, or so I felt. I stood utterly undone. Never had I ever felt so exposed yet so strangely covered at the same time! A moment had come, a moment I longed for and yet never truly expected! No words were spoken, but I knew instinctively I was being given a second chance—a last chance—and somehow it came through this Jesus! But how was this possible?

The curtain of people closed the gap, breaking the glance holding me spellbound, but I stood as still as a deer—lost in the moment, still feeling those piercing eyes searching in the depths of my heart. Only seconds had slipped by, but it felt like a lifetime. I unquestionably felt that somehow he offered me an open door, a way to break free from the weight of lies and lust that held me captive. I knew that if I accepted, there was no going back, *ever*, to the way I'd lived; and if I didn't, misery would wash me daily with her tainted brush!

Jesus had apparently ended his speech, for the crowd surged forward to follow him up the stairs. Hoping desperately for another glimpse of him, I stumbled along with them but stopped short of the wide open doors. Everything inside me wanted to rush after him, but I dared not follow; the priests wouldn't hesitate to throw me out of the temple. So I stood alone, watching the mob melt away through the entrance.

Strangers passing by cast curious glances as I hovered irresolute on the stairs. Unconsciously I pulled the folds of my cloak further across my face. Recognition was the last thing I wanted, for I was facing a defining moment and I needed to choose well. But first I had to be certain that I'd read this earth-shattering possibility correctly.

Perhaps if I wait I'll get an opportunity to speak to him. After what has passed between us, surely he will not reject me. It was more a question than a certainty, for it was impertinent to hope for such an interview. Then, preparing for a long wait, I moved over to the low wall skirting the building and sat down deep in thought, my morning's errand at the market forgotten.

I longed to be set free, but now that it was offered so simply, could I be? Did freedom really only take believing in this man and that he was indeed the son of God? Would I really not perish but have everlasting life? And what about my guilt, this heavy burden that constantly condemned me, would that be lifted off me as well? Is that what he meant by the words "For God did not send his son into the world to condemn the world but to save the world through him?" What if I do believe in him, that he is God's son, what then? Will this belief in him change my need for relationships that offer only a momentary respite from loneliness? Is it really that easy to be free of these heavy chains that have held me captive for so long? What if I try and fail? The questions felt endless, and the uncertainty even worse. *I'm scared, so scared*! I thought, and quailed under yet another onslaught of doubt.

Time dragged her heels while the strengthening sun effortlessly shifted position, benevolently shedding its life giving rays. Who is he? Is he really the son of God, and can he truly free me from sin? What if this is just another illusion? The unanswered questions linked into each other, forming a long chain of uncertainty even as the intensity of conviction faded. *I have to speak to him*, I thought, shifting uncomfortably on the hard seat. *I have to be sure he does hold the key I need to unlock the door to freedom. What can be keeping him, and what if he fails to recognize me?* I dismissed this last thought abruptly; in that case none of this strange hope was real!

The cloak slipped backwards unnoticed. I absently caught the eye of a Pharisee as he approached, and I blushed with shame at his look of leering disgust. *What if a vulture like that is with Jesus?* At the horrid thought the hair on my arms stood up. Was it too much to hope that he would be alone?

At last Jesus appeared, surrounded by not one but a flock of insatiable Pharisees, all loudly pounding him with questions. Another docile group of men, obviously disciples, followed a few feet behind. From nowhere people appeared and tried to touch him, while the Pharisees, acting as self-appointed bodyguards, shoved them aside. *Is he never alone?*

I wondered, desperate for his attention and tasting blood as I bit my lip in frustration. *How can I catch his eye?*

Suddenly he came closer. This was my chance! I began to stand when the man who'd earlier recognized me took hold of his arm, stopping Jesus within three feet of me. I shrank back onto the half vacated seat and huddled under the cloak's protection, fighting fresh waves of shame. This was not the time to approach him ... not now!

How dare he rob me of my only chance of speaking to him? I blazed inwardly.

The Pharisee, unaware of any offense, spoke my own thought. "Teacher, my associates and I have many more questions. This is really not the time or the place to ask them." Here he paused and gestured at those about him. "We were wondering if you would care to join us for dinner tonight at my residence."

After a short pause Jesus graciously accepted the invitation. When questioned as to whether he knew the address, he politely assured the Pharisee that one of his disciples knew the way.

Well, so do I; this then is my chance. I will also come tonight and intercept Jesus just before he reaches the house!

The top of the hill opposite the Pharisee's estate was cast in deep shade by the setting sun, and here, behind a bush, I crouched. It was impossible to come any closer without being seen, and I couldn't risk being noticed and then chased away. Nevertheless, it was a good hiding place, for the road sweeping up from the town on the right of me was plainly visible, as was the wide and pleasing entrance to the courtyard in front of the elegant house. Down below, servants scurried about like dark, shadowy beetles across the rough patio slabs. Oil-lamps were set out and water jars filled as they busily prepared for the arrival of the guests.

I looked to the right; presently, a group of men came into view. I watched their rapid approach anxiously, but the dusky light made recognition from this distance too difficult. Soon they would walk by the leafy hedge, rustling in the breeze beneath me, and then it would be easier to identify them.

All birds of prey, I decided, using my favorite metaphor for the religious leaders as they came by, oblivious of scrutiny. Servants sprang forward to usher them into the court and perform the ceremonial cleansing of their feet before leading them into the bright room peeping invitingly beyond the ornate entrance.

A well-dressed Pharisee came out to greet them, and I instantly recognized their host. The man formally greeted each with a kiss before they were escorted into his comfortable home. A little bored with these activities, I gazed up at the deepening sky.

He's cutting it rather fine, I thought impatiently, fingering the gift I'd brought along. Mystified I scanned the barren road. No-one else for miles about was in sight! I glanced casually the other way and stared in horror at a small huddle of men rapidly approaching from that direction.

"It can't be them, can it?" I gasped. "That's not the direction from town!'

My goal was to speak to Jesus before he arrived at the courtyard. If he was among these people, then this aim would be impossible to achieve, for I could never reach him before a servant did. Even as I stared, the gap narrowed. Then I saw him!

Perhaps if I run I can beat the servants, I thought frantically.

Casting caution to the wind, I slipped from the shadows and began to sprint full tilt down the short hill, only to be brought up short, breathless and staring. The host, having abandoned his guests, had reached Jesus ahead of the servants. And now, with his hand tucked firmly under Jesus' arm, was leading him unceremoniously into the house!

Thwarted again, I stood for a few shocked seconds absorbing this unprecedented lack of respect. Fortunately for me, the servants were too pre-occupied with the activities to notice my rapid descent. Suddenly, my legs gave way and I crumpled down onto the grass, watching helplessly as the remaining guests, one after another, were escorted inside until only the servants remained. My flimsy hope of deliverance was rapidly disappearing with each new and unexpected development.

Perhaps the meal won't take too long. I could wait until he comes out, or watch for another opportunity. But what if that never happens? I pondered, caught-up in a bind of indecision.

"Oh God, what shall I do?" I moaned in sick despair to the vast inky blackness above, feeling small and forgotten, like a stray thread sticking out annoyingly from the neat and ordered fabric of society.

Slowly I became aware of something pressing between my thigh and calf. Automatically my hands felt for and found the offending object. It was the gift I meant to give him. Then, an extraordinary idea birthed—an idea so amazing, which challenged tradition in every sense, that I caught my breath.

Perhaps there was a way! Perhaps God was answering me, showing me the way forward. Now the question was: could I do it? Did I have the courage to brave the vulture's nest and face the derision of his guests for a man I'd only briefly glimpsed for the first time that morning?

"Can I do it? Can I?" I whispered to nothing but silence about me.

The wind, the only observer of my dilemma, nodded the leaves above my head as I stared expectantly up at the stars, awaiting an answer from that vast array of silent and twinkling witnesses to God's omnipotent power.

The astonishing and quite unfamiliar sense of oneness with God increased, and I decided that if this was the cost for me to begin correcting the mess I'd made of my life, then I would do it!

I stood up, shook the dusty grass off my gown, and crept stealthily down the slope to the courtyard. The snores of the sleeping servant guarding the entry, warning me like the constant ring of a bell where not to tread. I silently stepped past him and peered anxiously around the deserted court. From what I could see, it was empty of people. Gaining courage, I inched forward, but had barely gone more than a few steps when I stubbed my toe against an uneven slab and stumbled awkwardly. The slight noise disturbed the guard and he called out sleepily. I froze in panic. He must have seen me, for he yelled volubly for help. Clumsily, still half-asleep, he started up in pursuit, even as more servants appeared magically from out of the shadows. One of them made a grab for me, but I ducked out of the way and rammed into a water jar, sending it clattering noisily across the tiles.

The courtyard wasn't this big from the hill, I thought frantically as I sped across, narrowly avoiding another servant's dive. I raced for the beckoning, welcoming light shining through the open doorway and collided headlong into the host coming out. Springing free, I tripped and fell backwards into the wide reaching grasp of a servant close behind me. His arms were like rods of iron pinning me suffocatingly.

The master of the house pulled off the hood roughly, uncovering my bent head, and we glared at each other—he angrily, and I like a trapped animal with a wild defiance born from fear. Then his eyes lit in recognition and the dangerous expression altered strangely. Quite unexpectedly, he ordered my release.

"Do you wish to see the teacher?" he asked perceptively and impatiently.

I nodded nervously. For an instant he looked immensely pleased. Then with a sinister smile he stepped aside so I could pass. When I hesitated, the smile fell off his face like bark peeling off a tree, leaving it inflexible and hard. I realized that I had no other choice but to follow the hand that motioned me to go ahead of him into the house. As I passed, he gripped my arm and together, like sleep-walkers in a peculiar dream, we walked through the entrance into the well-lit and spacious room beyond.

Immediately, much of the conversation ceased as heads twisted and turned to stare, even as the Pharisee let go of my arm. All except one. He remained reclining at the table with his back to me. Feeling rather like an actor who with a sudden start overcomes stage-fright, I crept forward until I came up behind him. Now that I was this close, I could feel the power emanating from him, and I knew unquestioningly that all he'd said about himself was true. Overcome with emotion, I fell down at his feet, sobbing.

Jesus did not try to stop me, nor did he cringe or pull away; instead, he let me cry on. Then I noticed his feet were wet with tears and I kissed them tenderly. After that, I undid my long coil of hair and mopped them carefully. Taking the flask of perfume from my pocket, I poured this liberally over those precious feet.

As I worshipped at his feet, I heard him address the Pharisee. Startled, I looked up, for I had utterly forgotten the man. He must have followed me, for he was standing close by.

"Simon, I have something to tell you."

"Tell me, teacher," he prompted smoothly, a mocking smile twisting his lips as he appraised me with disgust.

"Two men owed money to a certain moneylender. One owed him five hundred denarii, and the other fifty. Neither of them had the money to pay him back, so he cancelled the debts of both. Now, which of them will love him more?"

"I suppose the one who had the bigger debt cancelled," he replied grudgingly, the smile quickly fading as the question's intent hit home.

"You have judged correctly," Jesus said, gesturing towards me. "Do you see this woman? I came into your house. You did not give me any water for my feet, but she has wet my feet with her tears and wiped them with her hair. You did not give me a kiss, but this woman from the time I entered has not stopped kissing my feet. You did not put oil on my head, but she has poured perfume on my feet. Therefore I tell you, her many sins have been forgiven, for she loved much. But he who has been forgiven little loves little."

I glanced shyly down and blushed rosily at this praise. No-one had ever said anything quite so special about me.

Then Jesus said to me, "Your sins are forgiven, your faith has saved you; go in peace." As I went, understanding lit up those wonderful words and I gasped. I, a wicked woman who had abandoned real love for a very poor substitute, had been commended by the son of God for loving well!

"God help me not to disappoint him," I prayed fervently, for I felt clean and whole, as though someone had taken off the dirty clothes of shame that clung perpetually in rags about my worn and battered spirit and dressed me in a dazzling, spotless and costly garment, designed by the most renowned couturier ever.

The Gift

*"Those who look to him are radiant;
their faces are never covered with shame."*
—Psalm 34:5

The tightly packed rows of stone benches circling the low wooden platform were filling fast with an odd assortment of people, from the roughest to the most sophisticated, when the woman arrived to take her place. She was positioned on the far corner of the stage, affording her a view of the congregation on the left and an ominous line-up of ornate and still empty chairs, commonly known as the "chief seats," on the right.

Even though the auditorium was large, the space felt oppressive and airless, and the woman unconsciously waved a hand to cool her face as she gazed routinely around. Resignation was wrapped like a garment about her to the point where she felt utterly detached from the proceedings, a spectator instead of a key player.

"The crowd has come for blood, and they'll get it, too," she reflected calmly, experiencing a fleeting thankfulness that she was not jammed between the heavily breathing and sweaty bodies while she watched them cram onto the seats with an air of impatient and rowdy expectation.

A noise akin to a cheer erupted from the packed gathering as the elders began to file past. The woman sat idly watching them—the rulers in extravagant tunics and turbans, strutting with importance, and the priests in long gowns of blue, fringed with small golden bells alternating with pomegranate tassels in blue and purple and scarlet yarn. The gowns rustled impressively as they marched purposefully over to the other side of the podium. For a brief moment she was reminded forcefully of sour vinegar as a waft of sweaty air, disturbed by the rapid movement, reached her nose, which she wrinkled in quick distaste. Soon, sharp, scraping sounds of wood on wood rent the air as the rulers and priests settled noisily into the straight-backed chairs.

"Their faces tell the same story," she muttered under her breath, staring at the set, determined features void of all emotion. "This trial is merely a screen for justice; the verdict has already been decided."

Surprisingly, this realization did not ruffle her composure. She felt strangely prepared for this moment coming, even as it did, so many years after the last.

One of the Pharisees stood up and walked over to the pulpit standing in the centre of the raised platform. The crowd stilled as he began loudly to announce the charges. Then he called for the first witness to come to the stand. The woman sat a little straighter, craning her neck to get a better view as he stepped forward.

It was the man she expected, but not the man she remembered. His straight shoulders had hunched. A paunch sat untidily about the slim hips, and his thick dark hair had changed to thin wisps of grey. Only the profile remained the same. Age had reduced him to a mere shadow of his former handsome self. Gasps of shocked surprise and cries of amazement rippled like waves through the room as much of the populace recognized him. One of the elders stood up and rapped on the floor with his stick, calling for order even as the witness, with ashen countenance, stepped stiffly onto the stage to respectfully face the elders.

"How crushed he looks; he must feel like a rat caught in a trap. The Pharisees must have forced him to testify. I wonder what he'll say," she whispered beneath bated breath, feeling one with the engaged multitude.

The Pharisee who'd opened the proceedings motioned for him to begin as rapt silence enveloped the congested and humid room. The witness bent his head and swallowed uncomfortably. He was silent for a moment, his mouth taut and thin as he struggled for composure. A chair close to where the woman sat quietly watching shifted impatiently, noisily, attracting his attention. He automatically glanced over in that direction and caught her eye. Both started uncomfortably. Then, for a brief, betraying instant his look hardened before he quickly turned away, and she paled a little.

His words were at first slow, almost hesitant, but it soon became plain that he was choosing them with care. Before long they rang out authentically as he drew in the crowd with a fantastic tale of the scene she remembered so well, as if even he were fully convinced that he was the victim of a vile and calculated seduction. The connection she felt with the crowd severed irrevocably as they whistled and yelled encouragement, enjoying every twist of the scandalous fabrication.

As his claim unfolded, she stared, incredulous—and, as she stared, something tender within withered and died, destroying any lingering illusions she had over him. She found it odd to imagine that she was once so trusting, so intimate with the man. He was a total stranger now. Then, with some surprise, she found she wasn't angry; instead, the only feelings she had were ones of pitying disillusionment.

"God help his soul," she murmured and sighed, aware of a deep disappointment when he finally left the witness stand and walked shamelessly and, almost self-righteously, back to his seat, even as another witness was called forward.

How different this trial is from the other, she found herself thinking as the examination of an eyewitness dragged on. That time her heart had pounded like an over-sized drum when some of these Pharisees, who were now sitting judging her today, cornered her, like a pack of ravenous wolves, in that compromising moment of intimacy. Then they hauled her, kicking and screaming, through the streets, their cruel fingers digging deep into the soft, bare flesh on her arms. At the temple they thrust her before a teacher, disrupting his session. Every nerve in her body screamed its outrage at being made an object for the curious to gawk at. She struggled like a wild cat to get free, but was forced to submit and stand exposed before him and the others. Then one of those self-appointed adjudicators, while blatantly leering at her, pointed an accusing finger and shouted:

"Teacher, this woman was caught in the act of adultery. In the Law, Moses commanded us to stone such women. Now what do you say?"

The contemptuous sneer in the Pharisee's tone was unmistakable—unmistakable enough to make her forget her humiliation and stare at this strange judge of judges, seated quietly amid the silent watchful assembly.

Who is on trial here? she wordlessly wondered. Every eye was fixed on the stranger, but he barely moved a muscle as he sat staring thoughtfully down at the ground. Then he glanced swiftly up, his eyes instantly meeting hers. That cool, thoughtful and remarkably pure look shook her to the core, and she shivered despite herself.

The silence in the courtyard was tangible, the seconds like hours as she waited for him to proclaim the sentence, to denounce her even as the Pharisees. Instead, he bent over and began to write with his finger on the ground. A couple of disgusted Pharisees snarled out accusations again, trying to force a response, but managed instead to work up some of the bystanders. They responded by picking up stones and cursing. Only the man remained utterly unmoved.

How he fascinated her. What did he write, and how did he gain the Pharisees unwilling and hostile respect? How did he do it? He was so ordinary and surprisingly young, yet his control over the crowd complete. There was nothing exceptional about him, nothing except the expression within his eyes. Then he straightened, and the restless horde instantly quieted. His sweeping gaze absorbed them all before he addressed them directly.

"If any one of you is without sin, let him be the first to throw a stone at her."

The words were so unexpected that it took almost a minute before she fully understood their meaning. The religious leader's frustration became instantly palpable, and her arms throbbed with bruising pain. Some of the watching men grumbled and swore obscenely under their breath. The mood became tense and unpredictable, but the man just sat quietly writing on.

All eyes were drawn, grudgingly, to that calm, quiet writing until, slowly, those closest to him, one by one after reading what he had written, began to leave like frustrated vultures when the carrion has been removed. First the elders left, and then the others, and before long they'd all gone, even those who'd held her captive, until it was only the two of them.

The man then straightened and looked up. "Woman, where are they? Has no one condemned you?"

"No one, sir," she replied.

"Then neither do I condemn you. Go now and leave your life of sin," he answered.

The penalty of death had been dropped, but the sweet pardon came with a price tag, and one which she couldn't fully pay, try as she might, for the desire to sin clung like a curse. After that day, however, she questioned many about him. Most believed he'd come to free them from the tyranny of the Romans, and so, caught up in the same bubble of excitement, she joined the procession waving palm branches, shouting hosannas, and hailing him as the long-awaited Messiah on the day he rode a donkey colt into Jerusalem.

How little she understood!

Then came *that* day, that dreadful day, when she stood looking up at his awful blood-spattered, mangled, and utterly unrecognizable body as it hung on a cross, silhouetted so crudely against that bleak, black sky. Nothing made sense then.

"How could you allow this, God? How could you? How could you allow them to kill him?" she screamed heavenward as she beat her chest to somehow ease the hurting. Never before had she felt so utterly crushed by the meaninglessness of everything.

Some other grieving women, one of whom was his mother, gathered around and invited her to stay with them. Eventually she joined in their prayer meetings. Then, unexpectedly, the spirit of God fell on them all with leaping tongues of fire, and finally understanding came. The words Jesus spoke to the apostles, "Shall I not drink the cup the Father has given me?" and of Isaiah, the prophet, "But he was pierced for our transgressions, he was crushed for our iniquities; the punishment that brought us peace was upon him, and by his wounds we are healed," suddenly made sense.

He came, not to free them from the tyranny of the Romans, but to drink obediently from that awful cup of suffering his father set before him, so that by allowing his sinless life to be a guilt offering for all, he could offer mankind the free gift of salvation. Jesus, the son of God, did not abandon her as she thought, but, besides pardoning her of adultery that day, later paid in full the price-tag of sin still owing on her life.

What a gift he gave her—not just a reprieve of her life here on this earth, but the dignity to stand, eternally free of the curse of sin and death, before God the Father! Her eyes filled with tears. Yes, how differently she saw his death now, the unbearable death that paved the way for her to receive eternal life.

A sudden uproar in the courtroom as the last witness sat down abruptly ended these thoughts. The Pharisees were now standing in a tight knot of unity. One of them stepped forward to give the verdict, motioning to the crowd for silence. Then he spoke, the sound piercingly harsh and cold.

"The court has found this woman guilty of belonging to the sect they call Christians, the group that have broken the Law of Moses, following after their own base instincts and forfeiting their inheritance in the family of Abraham, even as Esau so carelessly tossed aside his birthright for a mere pot of stew. Furthermore, she has shamelessly, using the same secret skills of the ancient Amorite women, enticed an innocent man to have intimate relations with her, even as this witness has testified." Here the Pharisee paused to catch his breath and point at her ex-lover.

"She is the worst kind of woman, a cheating, conniving Jezebel, and a heretic, and is not fit to live in our Jewish community. We are commanded by our father Moses to eradicate, from our society, this progeny of Eve, and we therefore pronounce, according to the law, the purging punishment of death by stoning."

The judgment she was once reprieved of, had come; the religious leaders finally had their way!

A low growl erupted into a loud volcanic rumble as the hostile crowd rose up as one, shaking fists, craving justice. Some started to hiss, while others spat their urgent need. Then, like the signal of a trumpet, a loud and vulgar shriek caused them all to surge forward in a tidal wave of inescapable screaming profanity.

Terror gripped her, shredding the detached calm, as she took in this boiling pot of humanity spilling over and up to where she stood. She raised a cold, shaking hand to steady an uncontrollably quivering upper lip. Where was Jesus? Was he still with her? It was hard to tell with her heart thumping so fast and her body shivering as it did.

Two guards on either side of her grabbed hold of a trembling arm and yanked her out of the frenzied courtroom and into the large open courtyard outside where she was swiftly released. She had barely enough time to take stock of her surroundings before she found herself hemmed in by half-crazed, animal-like faces. There was nowhere to run. She froze, mesmerized by the maddened and snarling crowd armed now with heavy rocks.

Suddenly within she clearly heard a voice say, "Precious in the sight of the Lord is the death of his saints." Just as instantly, a bright light, unseen by all but her, appeared, and she cried with pure delight, causing the startled mob to fall back a few paces. Jesus, with hands held out, was beckoning her. He had come! He was with her! She reached out her arms and stepped forward even as the rabble, howling in wild fury from what cause they knew not, surged again. Something sharp and hard hit her, and she cried out in pain, instinctively protecting her head, as stone after stone pelted down, forcing her backward. An extra hard blow knocked her clean off her feet, and she crumpled over, cracking the base of her skull on a discarded shingle.

Rocks continued to rain down and dress the still figure in a funeral gown of crushed stone while the wide-open and lifeless eyes stared fixedly, serenely up at an untroubled blue heaven.

Wells of Water

> *"For it is by grace you have been saved,*
> *through faith—and this not from yourselves,*
> *it is the gift of God."*
> —Ephesians 2:8

"How typical of a man!" muttered the younger woman glaring resentfully at the hefty frame of a man in his prime of life who lay sprawled and snoring on the floor, blissfully unaware of the hostile stare absorbing every detail of his dishevelled body. "Instead of working through your feelings, you go off and get plastered! And now, when there is work to be done, you are out for the count, sleeping off the binge," she vented. She felt stretched to the end of her limits, like water that has reached the boiling point and has to let off steam. The man grunted as if in agreement, startling the woman, but it was only a false alarm. The heavy breathing resumed and she relaxed. Almost instantly her disgruntled thoughts, like a flock of cooing doves, settled again on the savage fight of the night before.

"It was unnecessary, just like all the other fights," she whispered indignantly, still addressing his comatose form. "If only you had said something, anything, earlier; how different it would have been. But no, you are too stubborn! The least little thing would have made such a difference, but to say nothing, nothing at all ..."

The minutes ticked away as she stared broodingly at the spent body, an angry frown crinkling her normally smooth alabaster brow.

"You knew what I was getting at, and if you, at the very least, had just acknowledged the incident, nothing would have happened. Instead, you kept maddeningly quiet and distant," she continued accusingly, blinded to the fact that any acknowledgement of his at that point in the argument would have been like a flame to dry wood.

Now that the need to rant was temporarily satisfied, the feeling of uncertainty that plagued her lately returned, gnawing away at her sense of well-being like vinegar on teeth. She abruptly turned from the man to gaze sightlessly out the window.

"I gave you every possible opportunity, even mentioned the friend who was with you at the time," she murmured angrily, "and you had known what I was about, that I knew. You said so later during the fight. Why did you have to play with my feelings until I couldn't stand it any longer, until I was forced to challenge you outright? And then to say so very casually— *too* casually, that the girl meant nothing?"

The knot in her stomach tightened. It was too little, too late. The threatening sparks of jealousy and suspicion had leapt into full-blown flame and, in a flash, she laid into him. This had thrown him into a foul mood and he, in turn, had torn strips off her with an even fouler tongue, when all she wanted was for him to allay the maddening insecurity and put his arms tenderly around her.

"Men are such fools!" she muttered bitterly, throwing another dark look his way.

The yelling match had been fierce; cruel words that should never have touched air were tossed back and forth, until the molehill became an immovable mountain. Then suddenly, livid with anger, he left the house and she sought refuge in bed. Later, much later, she heard him stumble about while ranting furiously at the mute walls. A big man in an ugly frame of mind would have scared even the stoutest heart, and she hugged the covers, wondering fearfully when it would end.

Fortunately, the wine took action and he keeled over dead drunk.

Why didn't you just say something, for surely my jealousy was clearly obvious? She cast another derisive look at the sleeping man. *Why did you have to string me along as though you had something to hide? Did I touch a nerve, some struggle over feelings that you have for this woman that you don't want me to know?* Her stomach muscles contracted again.

"I'm tired of these silly games we play, of the constant insecurity; it's so meaningless," she murmured. "Surely there must be a different way to live, a better way to do things. I need something lasting, something stolid that won't cave on me."

She leaned out the window and studied the sky. Judging from the position of the sun, it was almost lunch-time. She didn't feel at all hungry, just thirsty, and she poured herself some water from an almost empty jar. She grimaced as she sipped the lukewarm water.

"It's hot today. You'll wake soon and then you'll be very thirsty," she mused, watching him turn restlessly. "I'm not sure I'm in the right frame of mind yet to deal calmly with the bear of a head you'll have when you get up. All I want to do is go somewhere quiet where I have space to think."

She thought of the well. No-one would bother her there at this noon hour. It was the perfect place to be alone to think. She picked up the empty water jar, suddenly feeling lighter, freer. The well had always been for her a place of refuge. She didn't quite know why, perhaps it was because the well belonged so long ago to Jacob, and somehow that connected her to distant spiritual roots. Whatever the reason was, she could find peace and quiet there and get a fresh perspective on things.

The sky was pale and hazy and the air hot and motionless in the colorless heavens. Even the flowers that sprinkled the pathway appeared dull.

"Everything's familiar and boring," she thought heavily as she stared at the jaded landscape. "Dreary and boring … like us! Have we reached the beginning of the end?"

A lump constricted her throat. It was too unbearable to think on. Was it possible they were back in that awful place, where rigid pride destroys love? She sighed, feeling some of the anger frizzle away. Deep down she knew that no matter how bad things got, she didn't want it to be over.

Nothing stirred, and she could hear the sound of her feet crunching the thin, crusty layer of dry sand left behind by the long-since evaporated dew. The still air suddenly beat with the swooshing sound of many wings. She glanced up to see a handful of low flying crows passing overhead. She stopped to watch them, glad of the feathery distraction. They changed direction and flew upward, making large repetitive loops as they circled high in the sky above until gradually, with every fresh loop, they dropped lower. Their target soon became apparent. A loud twittering erupted from the clump of trees away to the left as the nesting pairs became increasingly disturbed by the approaching predators.

Suddenly, the air was filled with loud and angry squawking as a myriad tiny swallows, with lightning quick dives and fierce precise pecking, assaulted the larger birds. The crows were forced to beat a hasty retreat, and they were chased high up into the opaque sky. Once free of the minute missiles, the affronted birds let loose a volley of frustrated squawks before swiftly nose-diving down again. The swallows immediately rallied and assumed their defensive assault once more. This pattern of attack, repel, and chase continued for a while longer until the crows, utterly outmaneuvered by their formidable though diminutive foe, gave up the hunt and flew on to stalk easier prey.

That'll teach these big bullies they can't always intimidate those smaller than them, she thought passionately. *That's what love is like—just one big pecking game with the strong swooping down on the susceptible, sweeping aside their weak defenses, having their fill and then seeking new pastures to conquer. At least for me it is,* she thought dejectedly. *I'm an easy target! I give in too easily to a man's charm, and then he tears my heart out and tramples on it. What I need is a stronger defense.*

She laughed sourly. "I think I'm getting a bird's eye view on how to deal with two-legged predators." She glanced down and noticed a fine layer of dirt coating her feet. "*Dirt,* that's what he called me. What right has he? He's as much *dirt* as I am!" Derision fanned alive another burning ember on the dying residue of pain and anger.

"Why does he have to taunt me so? Does belittling me make him feel less guilty because he's contemplating an affair with this woman? Or is he just trying to prove his independence and that he can still do what he likes? He knew how I'd react, that I wouldn't take even a hint of unfaithfulness lying down!" Her animosity intensified. "What a big, stupid idiot he is to go and get so drunk! Anyway, how dare he drag my past relationships into our fight and contemptuously call me names! He's no different than me; I've only had five other partners, while he's had many more! Doesn't he realize that men also become disreputable after multiple relationships?"

She kicked at a random pebble and watched with some satisfaction as it flew high into the air and landed some yards away.

"That'll teach you to get out of my way in future," she scolded the inert stone sharply as she passed the spot where it lay.

She spent the next few minutes absorbed in looking, with some perverse pleasure, for another inanimate victim. After finding no suitable stone, she abandoned the quest. Her shoulder began to complain about its burden, so she shifted the water pot to the other shoulder in an attempt to balance the weight.

Life is such a pointless cycle of constant daily grind, she thought resentfully. *I have to keep collecting water and cook food and clean house and wash clothes for the two of us, and what do I get in return? A fight over some other woman! Is it really so hard for us to withstand temptation? Are we really that fickle?* she wondered dully. Her ankle brushed against a stray weed and dislodged an ant which crawled quickly onto her foot. She bent over to flick it off, ingested some loose, swirling dust, and spat angrily on the ground in disgust.

Perhaps mankind could only love well in the beginning, when Adam and Eve were perfect and hadn't yet succumbed to sin. Since then it has been one long, sad story of betrayal after betrayal. What we need, she thought longingly, *is the Messiah to come and sort it all out for us!*

Jesus surveyed the quiet countryside stretching peacefully down toward the distant outline of huddled buildings. There was not a soul in sight, his disciples having vanished long ago on their errand to procure food. Only the bowed heads of grain, heavy with seed, paid him homage. He must be a little early for today's appointment, so he stretched out his tired legs as he settled down near the edge of the well to wait. The journey over the past days had been long and arduous, and although the day was only at its prime, the much needed rest was welcome.

He shifted about on the rough surface to get more comfortable and knocked over a small stone. A faint whistling echo followed its decent down the smooth, dark cavern of wall before a distinct and clear *plop* was heard as it hit water. His gaze moved from the well's unreachable depths to the laden fields basking under the dry heat. The scripture verse, "*Jacob's well is secure in a land of grain and new wine, where the heavens drop dew. Blessed are you, O Israel!*" floated into his thoughts. He stared reflectively at the mature, eager grain.

"*Why do you say, O Jacob, and complain O Israel; my way is hidden from the Lord; my case is disregarded by my God?*" he quoted softly to the inquisitive ears of wheat rustling gently in the breeze towards him.

"*Listen to me, my people; hear me, my nation,*" he continued as the wheat bent closer. "*I tell you, open your eyes and look at the fields, they are ready for harvest.*" The heads of wheat bobbed knowingly as the words rippled gently in ever widening concentric circles over the full fields, through the parched air, towards the iridescent heat rising up from the dusty land.

Then he looked into the distance, at the shimmering outline of the undulating horizon. "*The poor and needy search for water, but there is none; their tongues are parched with thirst. But I, the God of Israel, will not forsake them. Do not be afraid, O Jacob, my servant, Jeshuran, whom I have chosen. For I will pour water on the thirsty land and streams on the dry ground, I will pour out my Spirit on your offspring, and my blessing on your descendants.*"

He glanced back along the path towards the town and saw the distant shape of a woman, an empty water jar poised casually on one shoulder, and a small cloud of dust puffing up about her feet as she made her way towards him. "*Come all you who are thirsty, come to the waters; give ear and come to me; hear me that your souls might live ... Let him turn to the Lord and he will have mercy on him, and to our God, for he will freely pardon.*"

He studied her silent approach along the wide path skirting the laden fields ready for reaping. "*Come to me all you who are weary and burdened and I will give you rest,*" he thought as he observed the dejected slump of shoulders and defiant, angry gait.

Yes, indeed the fields were ripe and ready for harvest, and he must be about his work, the work his Father had sent him to do.

Exasperation emanated from every line of her taut body as she strode up to the well and set down the jar with a thud upon the ground, tossing a fresh swirl of dry dust into the air. She sighed deeply with exasperation and, ignoring him, deliberately turned her back.

Why is this stranger here, and what right does he have to sit on my well and intrude on my space? The last thing I want to see right now is a man—any man! Is there no place free of them? she fumed inwardly.

Slipping the jar off her shoulder with one fluid, angry motion, she bent quickly and grabbed the rope that hung from the pulley. She curled the knotted end deftly over the wide mouth before yanking it tight and lowering the jar skillfully into the well. She felt desperate for some peace. Even as the jar splashed into the cool water far below, she'd made up her mind, as soon as the water was drawn, to go and find a shady and quiet spot under some trees. Jesus waited a few moments until her task was completed and then addressed her half-averted face.

"Will you give me a drink?"

Annoyance clothed every evenly proportioned feature as she turned to face him. She examined him from top to toe, absorbing his dusty weariness, noting for the first time that he was a Jew. Righteous indignation rose up inside at this discovery, overcoming any stray feeling of sympathy.

The impudence of the man; what all men want, she thought fuming, *are women serving them! And Jews are the worst! Normally they won't even speak to us lowly Samaritans, except as master to servant. Imagine a Jew, asking me, for a favour!* She said sharply: "You are a Jew and I am a Samaritan woman. How can you ask *me* for a drink?"

Jesus gazed steadily into her eyes. "If you knew the gift of God and who it is that asks you for a drink, you would have asked him and he would have given you living water."

She eyed him scornfully. "Sir, you have nothing to draw with and the well is deep. Where can you get this living water? Are you greater than our father Jacob, who gave us this well and drank from it himself, as did also his sons and his flocks and herds?"

Jesus chose to ignore the heavy sarcasm coating the questions like treacle. "Everyone who drinks of this water will be thirsty again, but whoever drinks of the water I give him will never thirst. Indeed, the water I give him will become in him a spring of water welling up to eternal life," he answered tolerantly.

She gaped at him. *The man must be mad,* she thought suspiciously. *Unless this is some bizarre attempt to hit on me.* She assumed a provocative stance and purred, "Sir, give me this water so that I won't get thirsty and have to keep coming here to draw water."

He looked at her intently. "Go, call your husband and come back."

She shifted uncomfortably beneath the intensity of the searching gaze, acutely aware of the fight she'd had earlier that morning with her lover, and began to feel ashamed of being so brazen.

"I have no husband," she replied sulkily.

Jesus said bluntly, "You are right when you say you have no husband. The fact is, you have had five husbands, and the man you now have is not your husband. What you have just said is quite true."

Her face flushed deeply and indignantly, and she glanced around suspiciously, half expecting to see some tell-tale informer. *There's no-one else here*, she thought in confusion, seeing only a small huddle of men approaching in the distance. A slight breeze gently stirred the grain, making their full heads nod as if in agreement.

Of course! He must be a prophet! I need to distract him, she thought cagily. "Sir," she said guardedly. "I can see you are a prophet. Our fathers worshipped on this mountain, but you Jews claim that the place where we must worship is in Jerusalem."

Jesus smiled, aware of her intention. "Believe me, woman, a time is coming when you will worship the Father neither on this mountain nor in Jerusalem. You Samaritans worship what you do not know; we worship what we do know, for salvation is from the Jews. Yet a time is coming and now has come when the true worshippers will worship the Father in spirit and in truth, for they are the kind of worshippers the Father seeks. God is spirit, and his worshippers must worship in spirit and in truth."

This irritated her; prophet or not, he had no right to make such outrageous statements as if he had a direct connection with God. Who did he think he was, the Messiah? And why was he trying to explain deep spiritual truths to her of all people?

Aloud she said with an edge of annoyance, "I know that Messiah is coming, and when he comes, *he* will explain everything to us."

Then Jesus declared candidly, "I who speak to you *am* he."

Astounded, she remained silent; for once not sure what to say.

The men she'd noticed earlier arrived and gathered silently and protectively around him, clearly wondering at the improper discourse. They eyed her warily, but still no-one asked, "What do you want?"

Their evident discomfort helped her overcome the intense awe this sudden revelation had brought. "Please stay a while longer while I fetch the others. They will want to talk to you. I'll be as quick as I can. I will leave my water jar so you and your disciples may drink from it while I am gone."

When he nodded assent she scampered away, her mind still trying to absorb this incredible revelation.

How could a day that began so badly turn out so well, she wondered. She, a Samaritan nobody, had just met the Messiah, and he knew all about her! Never before had anyone's words touched her so profoundly. That he was a prophet she did not doubt, but to announce that he was more than that, that he was actually the one they were all waiting for, was something else! And to choose to make this announcement to *her* of all people was even more amazing.

What will my friends and family think? I have to find them and tell them; I have to tell them or I think I'll burst. I wish I could fly! she thought passionately, frustrated by the clumsy limitations of feet.

The tight cluster of flat roofed buildings grew larger, and soon the path wound round to the wide-open gateway where the market was in full swing. She rushed wildly into the midst of the familiar noisy confusion and hollered loudly.

"Come see a man who told me everything I ever did. Could this be the Christ? Come, you have to meet him; he's waiting at the well."

All activity halted momentarily, and the startled townsfolk peered round to identify the source of their confusion.

"Come," she shouted, hurrying on, her activity strangely at odds with the still crowd. "Come see a man who told me everything I ever did. Could this be the Christ? Come back with me, or else you'll miss him; he's waiting at the well!"

The people stood their ground wondering, uncertain; perhaps she *had* met the Christ! They knew her well, and this behavior was not true to type.

"Come, you have to come," she called even more urgently when no-one budged. "I'll be back in a few minutes. There is another I have to fetch and then we can go together, for you *must* come. This man has the words of life, and I don't know how long he will stay," she cried desperately before darting through a door on the north side of the square, banging the adjacent wall in her haste.

Thank God he's still here, she thought, taking in the stationary man sitting at the table with his head buried in large work-worn hands. He cringed and lifted his face, revealing a scowl that stopped her dead in her tracks.

"Go away and make that racket elsewhere," he snarled, glowering at her from heavily puffed-up eyes, narrowed now to mere slits. When she didn't move or speak he sighed deeply in exasperation and gently nursed his head back into the comfort of those big and capable hands. Stepping quietly she crept closer, trying hard to suppress the intense excitement.

"I'm sorry for the noise," she began softly, apologetically, "but I've just spoken to a man who knew all about me, about *us!* The Messiah ..."

"I don't care if you spoke to God himself," he interjected weakly, removing a hand from its careful employment to wave her away. "Just go away!"

"But that *is* who I spoke to, *God's Messiah*, the one we've been waiting for! You have to come with me to the well and see for yourself; he has living water, the gift of life, you have ..." Her voice had raised a decibel from excitement.

"The Messiah? You?" The incredulous disgust sliced through the fast flowing words like a sharp knife, cutting her off in mid-sentence. She winced as if struck by some imaginary blow.

"Yes, the Messiah, do you hear?"she snapped defensively, bravely holding the livid, skeptical glare. "You must come quickly or you'll miss ..."

"If I didn't have such a rotten head, I would laugh!" he cut in crudely, sarcastically.

"Please listen; it is the Messiah!" she yelled, losing control, his need of quiet forgotten in the quick mercurial flash of fury. For a moment longer she met the blazing, red-rimmed eyes with an equally hot stare and then, with a sudden strangled sound, dropped her gaze as she sought desperately to bring under control the passionate intensity of feeling.

"Go away. Can't you see that I have a damnable headache? Go find someone else to tell your fables to and leave me alone," he growled sarcastically, the burning anger lighting his eyes cooling to a hard, malicious gleam as he watched her intense inner struggle.

She bit back another furious retort. He was baiting her again, and it would never do to fall into the trap again. Not now ... not today!

Mastering the rising emotion, she pleaded on. "Please come with me and see him for he has living water to give us, the words of eternal life ..."

"Oh, go away," he interrupted, his voice now icily distant. Deliberately ignoring her, he cradled his hurting head again.

She crept closer, her expression tender. "You have to come now or you might miss this chance to meet him!" she begged softly above the thick mop of hair covering the bowed head. Piercing, stony silence as loud as a verbally yelled "no" was the unyielding reply.

"Please, please come. He knows everything about me, about *us*," she insisted quietly, urgently. "The words of life are in him and he will teach us how to really worship God. I don't know how long he will hang around."

The broad shoulders braced and tightened, making the veins of the neck bulge. His head sank even deeper into the huge work-roughened hands for a brief moment. Then the chair grated roughly on the wooden floor as suddenly he lunged forward, his face twisted in ugly anger, stopped only by the sturdy table. His raised fist crashed down hard on the table top. His face instantly grimaced in pain as the thud reverberated through his taut, muscled body. She recoiled before him, her eyes widening from the threat; never before had he tried to hit her! His face reddened as he became aware that he had almost crossed a line.

"I have a splitting headache because of all the noise you've made with your stupid talk of Messiahs," he spat out furiously. "You push me too far, woman. I'm so angry with you."

She flinched. "I'm really sorry; I won't bother you anymore; I'll go at once. I only came back here to ask you if you wanted to meet God's Messiah with us. You will find us all at the well if you change your mind."

"You will do no such thing," he roared. "Don't you see how angry I am? First you ruin last night by accusing me of all kinds of things, and then you make the most awful racket, going on about some fake who has hoodwinked you into believing he is God. Now you want to walk out on me."

"I'm sorry I've made you so angry," she whispered unhappily, vaguely aware of a new and possibly insurmountable hurdle hovering between them, "but I must go. I promised Messiah I'd come back with friends and family, and when I called the others to come, I said I would bring them to him."

Ignoring her last comment, he stared irritably around the room and said angrily, "The place is a mess and I'm starving!" Then, in a pleading and slightly softer tone he added, "My head is really throbbing and I think I may throw up if I move about too much. You can help me by getting me some water and some food."

At this her mouth dropped open in dismay. "I will help you and get you a drink of water and prepare food for you as soon as I get back. I won't be gone long; I'll just take the others to him and fetch the water jar and then …"

"Even now you refuse to do what I ask. If he is God, then he would want you to obey me and help me," he responded touchily.

"I don't want to refuse you, but it's just not an ordinary day. The Messiah is here with living water, and … I have left the water jar at the well!"

"That was stupid, woman! Living water, huh? There's no such thing as living water!" he shouted and then winced again. With an effort he calmed himself. "Well, you can just go and borrow some water from a neighbor and fetch the jar later."

"I will help you, but I have to keep my commitment to him first."

"Listen, there is tension between us and I don't like it either; if you stay we can work this out. But if you don't stay and help me, I will know that you really don't care for me."

She stared at him, horrified by the unexpected twist in the association of his thoughts. "But I have to go, I promised …"

"I don't care what you promised, or to whom; if you go now, it will be the end of us!" he insisted coldly, stubbornly.

"But I have to go. He really *is* the Messiah! He has the words of life …"

"If you go, then you are choosing this imposter above me and my needs, and it will be over between us," he yelled.

"He's not an imposter. He knew all about us, about me. Don't you understand? I have to go! I may never see him again!" she cried desperately.

"Go out that door and our relationship is as good as over, for I won't change my mind."

This can't be happening, she cried inwardly as the awful chasm of misunderstanding widened between them. *There has to be a way to somehow stop this, to bridge this unbearable breach between us.* Aloud she said softly, "Please don't say that; I have to go. I have to! I have to keep my promise to him and to all the others. He really is who he says he is! If you could only meet him you would see that for yourself."

His eyes blazed anew. "I repeat—if you leave now, our relationship is over. I won't accept you back!"

She hovered irresolutely, her heart twisting in pain at the harsh demand. How could he force her to do this? How could she make such a choice?

"But what about the others? They need to meet him too," she cried piteously.

"I need you more. Let them go and find him by themselves; they don't need you."

"But I promised the Messiah I would come back." She stared sadly at him, still unable to fully grasp the awfulness of everything that was passing between them.

"Go out that door and I will never forgive you!"

Tears pricked as she stared mutely for a few moments at him, caught up in agonizing indecision. *How can you make me choose between you and the Messiah? How can you?* she screamed silently. Utterly unable to respond, she turned away. With leaden feet and a tear-heavy heart that dragged down her shoulders, she walked towards the open door.

Silence—cold unyielding silence—filled the room. At the door she threw him one last, lingering and utterly despondent glance. Then she quickly left.

Soon she and a bewildered but obliging crowd had gathered before Jesus. She listened to his life-giving words with a mixture of elation and heart-rending sadness. Never before had she experienced two such opposing emotions simultaneously. She found joy and peace in the new-found freedom he gave, but it came at a very high cost. After spending some time listening to him, the townsfolk urged him to stay with them. He remained for a further two days and because of his words, many more Samaritans became believers and said to her: "We no longer believe just because of what you said; now we have heard for ourselves, and we know that this man really *is* the savior of the world.

Afterword

I deliberately chose to place "Wells of Water" last in this little series of stories as ultimately all of us have the same choice to make, whether to believe on the name of Jesus, that he is the Messiah, God's only son, and accept the invitation to drink from the living water of his Spirit like the woman in this last story, or to refuse him like her lover. If you do choose to believe in the power of his name and accept his Spirit, I pray that it may not be as hard a choice as for this woman. If it does come with significant cost, however, then my prayer is that like the women in these stories, you will have the courage to endure the journey.

He said to me: "It is done. I am the Alpha and Omega, the beginning and the End. To the thirsty I will give water without cost from the spring of the water of life. Those who are victorious will inherit all this, and I will be their God and they will be my children."
—Revelations 21:6, 7